EXES & GOALS

Book 1 of The Slapshot Series

HEATHER C. MYERS

Chapter 1

THE NEWPORT BEACH SEAGULLS SUCKED. They used to have a legacy - no Stanley Cup yet - but they still had been a respectable team to play against. Once their founder, owner, and manager, Ken Brown, had been found murdered and one of his granddaughters inherited the team, everything fell apart. First, the captain - the one who happened to be dating Brown's older granddaughter, Katella - broke up with Katella and demanded to be traded after their home opener. Second, their goalie - Brandon Thorpe - was a suspect in the murder. Finally, Seraphina Hanson's inexperience running a business let alone a hockey team became apparent to the point where most of the players who became free agents ended up signing with other teams for a pay cut simply because they wanted to be on a team that was not tainted with controversy. Also, they wanted an opportunity to actually win a Cup and they did not believe that was going to happen with the Gulls.

Things needed to change.

Seraphina had a lot on her plate and a season under her belt. If she wanted to build a contending team, she needed to start with drafting and signing players that would help her do that.

Even if one of those players was involved his own sort of controversy.

"THANK YOU FOR COMING IN TODAY."

Harper Crawford sat in a plush office overlooking the Pacific Ocean. There were pictures in frames hanging throughout the room filled with family photos of sisters, of their grandfather, of their players. Even though Seraphina went to the University of California, Irvine and graduated cumme laude with a degree in Communication, her degree did not adorn one of the walls. It would not fit the sort of atmosphere she strived for when decorating her office - her grandfather's office.

Harper had never been in the office before. It was open, the desk made of glass so it was transparent. There was a thousand-dollar computer set up neatly on the surface with a tray filled with requests, memos, and paperwork. Her name plate with glass as well, with white loopy letters and the logo for the team engraved into the material. The chairs were the only dark furniture in the room - they were a black leather. Even the walls were white, making the office more open than it was. The carpet was a beige color. There was a red stain on it. Harper knew it was Ken Brown's blood. This was where he was murdered by his accountant. A lot of people who went in and out of Seraphina's office thought it was morbid to keep a blood stain when the family had enough to replace the entire carpet should they want to. But Harper knew Seraphina well enough to know the youngest granddaughter wanted it there as a reminder that her grandfather spilled blood because of this team. That he had been there. That he was still there. As odd as it sounded, it relieved Seraphina to see it every day.

"Sure," Harper said, her elbows resting on the arms of the

chair, looking at her friend with her head cocked to the side. "What's up?"

"We've known each other since college, right?" Seraphina asked.

Seraphina was beautiful in the way where she didn't know she was beautiful. She had wavy blonde hair and forest green eyes, with freckles splattered across her cheeks, giving the twenty-five-year old the look of youth rather than an experienced businesswoman. She wore a casual boyfriend shirt - this one maroon - tucked into a tight black high-waisted pencil skirt. On her feet, she wore shiny black four-inch heels with red soles. Her makeup was light but professional looking. It was weird - she was so different and yet exactly the same as the girl Harper knew from college.

She didn't know if the rumors regarding Seraphina and Brandon Thorpe - Newport Beach Seagull's starting goalie, Vezina-award nominee, and captain of the team - were true, that they were secretly dating, but if they were, Harper hoped he knew what a lucky man he was. Seraphina was sharp, educated, and familiar with the sport. If they weren't dating, Harper would be flummoxed. The two had chemistry and they seemed like they'd be a good match for each other. Seraphina had even come out, publically defending Thorpe when he became the primary suspect in her grandfather's murder. She barely even knew the guy. Of course, the media ridiculed her, claiming it was because of a love affair rather than just standing behind her teammates. Showing a steady stream of support when they needed it most.

"Do you still run your blog?" Seraphina asked. "The one on sport's writing? I followed it for a while last year, when we went on that run of six straight in a row but I stopped after..." She let her voice trail off and Harper didn't have the heart to finish it for her.

After they went on their subsequent losing streak, which lasted eight in a row, dropping them from a shaky .500 average to a .430 and crushing any hopes of making it to the playoffs as a wildcard. Not only that, they lost Fan Appreciation Night, which occurred as the last home game of every season.

The Newport Beach Seagulls sucked, but somehow, they always won Fan Appreciation Night.

Of course, the media ripped Seraphina for that one as well. Like it was her fault. And maybe, in part, it was.

Then, half the team left in the off-season, a couple of players retired, and she was scrambling to fill the holes. And she did. From what was being reported, she surprisingly acquired a decent team, at least on paper. It would be a different story to see if they actually had the chemistry to be a Stanley Cup Contender.

"I do," Harper replied. "I wouldn't necessarily say it's a sport's blog since it focuses on hockey but it does teach sport writing in generic terms."

"I want to hire you," Seraphina said, blindsiding Harper. But that was Seraphina for you; she was good at getting right to the point. "We've never had an official team blogger and God forbid someone actually wrote for the team rather than against us." She rolled her green eyes and the gesture made her look younger than her twenty-five years, which was saying something. "I can pay you a decent salary and you'll get benefits as well. Travel, hotels, all of that will be paid for. I just need you to write for the Gulls, about them. I don't want you coming across like a homer. I want you to be critical but I want you to always have our back, whether you're writing a character piece on a new player, a team practice, a community outreach event, you know."

"Wait," Harper said, blinking. The words hadn't sunk in yet. "You're going to give me a salary to write about the Gulls?"

"Yes," Seraphina said with a professional nod. "Of course, you won't just be writing about them. You'll be traveling with the team when they go on road games, you'll attend all of our community outreach events. You might be partnered with a couple of players throughout the year to write character pieces on them as well as the coaching staff. Think about it like you're going to keep a diary for the team as a whole. You're going to track where we started from and show how much we've grown. You're going to help keep track of all of our mistakes. You absolutely can offer solutions to those mistakes or you can interview coaches and players for their opinions. You'll be more than a blogger. You'll be like a record specialist for us."

"That sounds amazing," Harper began but caught herself. Her eyes dropped to her lap and she began to tug on her index fingers. "It's just..." She let her voice trail off and picked her eyes up so she could lock eyes with Seraphina. "I take care of my grandma. She lives by herself for now but I don't know how it's going to be if I'm traveling with the team."

Seraphina nodded, pressing her lips together. "So," she said after a moment of pensive thinking, "what you're saying is that she's your dependent?"

Harper tilted her head to the side. "I guess so," she said. "I take care of her every day, sorting her medication, taking her to her doctor's appointments, and run errands for her. I'm just worried if I'm gone for a week or two because of the road trips, something might happen. She'll take the wrong pill, she won't have food..." She let her voice trail off and gave Seraphina a sardonic smile. "I'm probably just overthinking things."

"Not at all," she replied. "I completely understand. Not that I had to take care of my grandfather by any stretch, but I completely get worrying about them and feeling responsible for their well-being." She crossed her arms over her chest but it wasn't a defensive gesture. "Would your grandmother feel comfortable if one of our on-call nurses checked in with her daily while you're gone?"

Harper's brow pushed up. She couldn't believe Seraphina was offering that. It meant more to her than she realized and she didn't know how to put into words the appreciation she was feeling toward the owner at that moment. That didn't mean her grandmother would be okay with a stranger taking care of her, of course, but it was something they might be able to work with if her grandmother was willing to get on the same page as her.

"I." Harper closed her mouth. She felt like a fish on land, trying to suck in air. "Yeah, I mean, I can ask her. I'm not sure how she'll feel about it but I'd be grateful for the opportunity."

"Of course," Seraphina said. "We would love to have you on the team."

Harper smiled because she wasn't quite sure how to respond.

"Do you have any questions for me?" Seraphina asked. Her voice was direct but warm, the type of voice that encouraged honesty.

Harper nodded. "Yeah, actually," she said. "What kind if pieces do you expect from me? Fluff pieces? Pieces that are notoriously bias toward the team?" She paused, hesitating only for a second. "I write hockey on my blog but I can be brutally honest about a team's performance."

"Trust me," Seraphina said with a grin. "I'm well aware of your honesty. I read what you wrote about our last season. It's exactly why I reached out to you, to be honest. As a woman and owner of a sports franchise, I'm tired of being the subject of fashion and diet articles, gossip about me saying a member of my team, and the fact that I don't know anything about hockey. Obviously you're not going to be writing about me, but when you did write about me, you didn't write about any of that. You wrote about everything as it directly related to hockey. And when we sucked - which we did the majority of the time - not only did you write about how we sucked, you offered solutions to our problems. I credit you to some of the changes I'm making around here, including creating this position. You're the only one I want for it." She leaned back in her chair. "So, to answer your question, I want you to write it all, as long as it's honest. I'll be giving you the majority of your assignments but if there's a topic or a player or something relating to the Seagulls that you want to run with, do it. I trust you."

Harper felt her lips curve into a smile and she nodded her head. "I can work with that," she said. "I appreciate the freedom."

"So is that a tentative acceptance contingent on your grandmother's approval?" Seraphina asked, her green eyes big and bright.

"Absolutely," Harper said.

Seraphina beamed, her entire face mirroring sunshine. She stuck out her hand and Harper leaned forward to shake it.

"Talk it over with your grandmother," Seraphina said. "Let's meet tomorrow after the press conference so you can sign paperwork and we can talk about your first assignment. I'll email you details about our medical benefits and the different options you qualify for. If everything is good and done, you'll start tomorrow. How does that sound?"

"Fabulous," Harper says, standing.

"Great." Seraphina stood as well. "I'm sure you heard but tomorrow I'm hosting a press conference in the parking lot here. I'll be introducing the new players and coaching staff. I want you to come."

"Absolutely."

Harper gave her new boss one last smile before turning and heading out of the office.

So this was what it felt like to walk on air.

Chapter 2

IT WAS the perfect day for a press conference. Summer in Newport Beach was warm with a cool sea breeze keeping things from being too unbearable. If Harper closed her eyes and focused, she could hear the nearby ocean crashing into the shore. As it was, there a group of fifteen people, representing the media that permeated the National Hockey League, chatting amongst themselves as they waited for Seraphina to make her announcement. The majority of the media were local - the Gulls didn't get a lot of national and international attention simply because they were still the newest team in the league and their play hadn't resulted in a playoff berth just yet. Also, the team could not seem to win more than half of their eighty-two games. They always fell short of a .500 season, which was laughable. Brandon Thorpe, the team's new captain and starting goalie, was the only reason why they were as competitive as they were.

Of course, the media had no problem devouring Seraphina in the news, calling her incompetent, a spoiled rich girl who had no idea how to manage a hockey team, and an embarrassment to the league. They had no issue resorting to blatant sexism, questioning her choice in clothing, reporting on her weight and hair styles, and even suggesting that women weren't as comparable in a position of power in a sports profession. It was absolutely infuriating.

As a writer of her sports blog, Harper decided had to write pieces about the coverage of Seraphina Hanson rather than the hockey team. Now, with Seraphina's job offer, Harper could still pretty much write whatever she wanted. And nothing would censor her unless it came directly from Seraphina herself.

Currently, Harper was seated in the third row of the five rows of white chairs put out specifically for the media. She had her recorder in the seat next to her, a pen in her left hand, and her notebook in her lap. She liked to take notes on top of recording because she could not predict when inspiration would strike and she always liked to be prepared. The press conference took place in the parking lot of Sea Side Ice Palace, the same arena where the Gulls played their games and practiced. It was unheard of, but Ken Brown also had public skating times and youth leagues that participated here as well. There were three rinks in the building total; the practice rinks were smaller and off in the back. There was even a special entrance for participants in the youth leagues so they felt like actual NHL players. Seraphina kept the tradition.

The lot was blocked off so the public could not enter, at least not during the press conference. As such, the number of cars in the lot were few and far between.

There was a simple podium that stood in front of the rows of chairs with a microphone already turned on and in position.

Harper glanced at her watch. Only a few more minutes.

Seraphina Hanson was always on time.

Harper felt her heart start to thump against the inside of her chest like pebbles skipping across the surface of the ocean. Her hand started to tap the end of the pen against her notebook in anticipation.

And then, Seraphina walked out of the building, her shoulders rolled back, her head held high. She looked like a super-model walking down the runway. Her hair billowed around her like a lion's mane and she walked with a swagger that could only be attributed to the jungle cat. All eyes were on her; people here were quick to criticize her, crucify her in their articles, but they were as in awe of her as Harper was. She wore a professional pantsuit with high heels - a white blouse that dipped low but not low enough to be deemed as inappropriate and grey slacks that clung to her curves before dropping to her ankles. On her feet were a pair of sleek black ankle boots.

When she got to the podium, she placed her hands on the edges and shot everyone a smile. Everyone quieted on their own; she didn't need to ask for their attention.

"Thank you," she said into the small black microphone, "for being here. We have a lot of ground to cover today, and I appreciate the fact that you're here to share all of this good news with me. As you know, we're taking the Gulls' in a new direction. We have some of our core key players but the majority of our team is new. Fresh. I'm hoping - we are all hoping - that this change will transform our team from abysmal to worthy."

Harper's eyes widened. Seraphina had called out her team's shortcomings without apology. It was rare for an owner, a general manager - hell, even a coach - to be so vocal regarding their team's struggles.

"Every year, we have fans that make a commitment to our team by purchasing season tickets," Seraphina continued. Harper had no idea how she was able to retain all of this information without needing flashcards. "We, in turn, make a commitment to play hard, play fast, and play on, regardless of the circumstances. We can't promise a win but we can promise effort. We can promise heart." She paused, letting her words hang in the air. Then, "Last year, we failed to honor our commitment to the fans. Which is why we decided to make some changes around here.

"Before I introduce the ten new members of this team, I

want to reassure the season ticket holders that last season was not something we're proud of. Here at the Gulls' organization, excellence is something we strive for because we know our fans expect it. Which they should. My grandfather's team will not be remembered for falling apart now that he's no longer here. I promise you that. I know I, along with every single person involved in some way, need to win your trust back. I will. We all will. Because you are important to us."

Seraphina glanced to her right where Harper noticed the coach and his team of assistant coaches. They stood there, all at varying heights, half of them with bushy mustaches, in white polo shirts with the Gulls' logo stitched to the left side of the shirt. They looked very uniform for simply being coaches, with brown belts and pressed khaki pants. At least they weren't wearing shorts. Seraphina didn't understand shorts at ice rinks. She didn't care how hot it was outside, it was a big fashion no - whether you were male or female.

She introduced each coach individually. With Henry Wayne retiring last year, Seraphina had to find a suitable replacement for him and his team. Luckily, Neil Cherney - a veteran player and former Seattle Raptors coach - was available and Seraphina swooped him up as soon as she could. It was one of her first moves in the off-season and one of the smartest. Cherney's record spoke for itself, though he was still underestimated in the league - first as a player and subsequently as a coach.

Once the coaches were through, Seraphina stepped back to the podium. "Now," she said, looking out at the media, "as I'm sure you know, we've acquired at least ten new players, some veterans of the league, some rookies, and we've brought some of our prospects up from San Diego to train with us and get a shot at making the final roster of the team. I'm going to introduce you to each one of them, starting with center Zachary Ryan."

Harper could feel the men around her tense and the photographers get in position, ready to take pictures. This was the moment they had been waiting for. There was a collective hush; everyone was holding their breath.

At that moment, he walked out, all six foot four of him. He was pure muscle and broad shoulders all compiled in a lean package. He had sandy blonde hair, short so nothing could fall in his face and inhibit his vision. He had crystal blue eyes and sharp facial features - high cheekbones, a strong jaw - and had a roughness about him that made him look more scruffy than handsome. But still handsome. He was wearing a polo with the Gulls' logo on it as well, but his was a sky blue, emphasizing his eyes even more than they already were, and dark blue jeans that fit him in all the right places. On his feet were a pair of expensive flip flops. He walked out of the Ice Palace with his chin up, his lips curled into a smirk. He walked with a confident swagger but he didn't come across as too arrogant.

When he got to the podium, he leaned against the surface and tilted his head down so his lips were close to the microphone.

"Hi," he said. His voice is low and masculine. "I'm Zach. I'm really happy to be here. I look forward to playing for the Gulls and start a new chapter in my career."

That was it. He straightened up as hands shot up to ask him questions. Harper kept hers to herself for now. She liked to wait and see what would be asked, how questions would be answered. He had a slight Canadian twang that she found she liked.

However, there was an arrogance in everything he did, an arrogance she wasn't sure how she felt about just yet. It could be either charming or frustrating. It could be both.

"Why did you choose the Gulls over the other teams you sat down with?" one of the men asked.

"Well, the environment is appealing," Zach replied. Harper watched as he directed his gaze at the journalist who asked the question, his sky blue eyes crystal and direct. "Who doesn't want to play in sunny Southern California?" He dropped his hands from the podium in order to use them to gesture along with his words. "There's also not as much pressure here. Hockey's not a popular sport in general here so the team can actually be big fishes in small ponds."

"So you're saying hockey isn't popular in Southern California?" another journalist asked.

Zach furrowed his brow, turning his attention to the female reporter. "Yes," he said. "I am. Look at the statistics: USA Hockey has only 25,000 plus people registered to play out of a state of thirty-six million. Hockey here is definitely growing and those that are fans are ravenous. They're the best kind of fans because the appreciation and understanding is there. But I don't have to worry about people recognizing me at the mall. I know some of the guys have kids who go to school here and all they are to the teachers and other parents is Dad. It's not a bad thing, honestly. I prefer it. It's one of the reasons why I decided to come here."

"Is it true you cheated on Diana Platt with some of the Toronto Bangles players' wives?"

They weren't in a room per se but the tension was tight and suffocating. Harper didn't know much about Zachary Ryan but he did seem to have a temper - not a bad one, exactly, but he wasn't afraid to tell you what he felt at any given moment. He was one of the players who chirped at the refs if he thought the ref made a bad call and he was one of the few skilled players who wouldn't back down from a fight if confronted unless, of course, the player was trying to goad him into taking a penalty and getting him off the ice.

"Honestly, I don't understand how my personal life has any relevance to my skills as a hockey player," Zach said. His tone was clipped but not confrontational. Harper could respect that.

"Have you changed your off-season workout regime to fit with the Gulls' expectations?"

Harper was already writing but she couldn't take her eyes off Zach. He was more attractive than she expected him to be, smarter as well. The question was inappropriate and completely out of line but he handled it somewhat professionally. She didn't know if she was going to ask a question. Right now, she wanted to get a read on him and see just the sort of man and player Zachary Ryan really was.

Chapter 3

HARPER HAD NEVER BEEN a nightclub type girl. She wasn't one of those girls who needed an excuse to wear a tight dress or one of those girls who thought dancing fixed everything. If she was stressed or needed a release, she grabbed an Xbox controller and played the latest Call of Duty game. It kept her focused and thinking solely about her mission - blow as much up as possible - and let her escape from the world for a few hours.

That didn't mean she was a tomboy. Far from it. She loved shopping for dresses and had a subscription to Cosmo she read religiously. She had a few fashion blogs she followed and developed her style into something that represented who she was. She loved shoes like any woman, and her shoe collection filled more than half of the tiny closet in her one-bedroom apartment.

Dancing, however, was not something she was privy to. Her body was too awkward and she felt like a fool, like everyone could tell she was pretending to be this cool girl who danced at nightclubs. She didn't fit in and she didn't want to.

However, Seraphina needed a character piece written about Zachary Ryan. "Honestly, we need to make him likable,"

Seraphina had told her in that meeting. "I want fans to care about him, not just that he's a first line type of player."

Harper agreed and Seraphina promised Katella would officially introduce the two of them that evening at Taboo, a nightclub located in Costa Mesa the single hockey players liked to frequent on their off days and the summers. Seraphina wouldn't be attending because she didn't want to mix with her employees. Also, if any news outlets found out she was partying with the players, her reputation would be crucified. Harper didn't think it was fair but Seraphina didn't seem to mind in the slightest and wished Harper good luck.

Harper and Katella discussed logistics and came up with a plan that consisted of Harper picking Katella up from the home she shared with her younger sister and driving the two of them to the club together. Also, Harper offered to be Katella's designated driver should the twenty-seven-year old need to indulge in comfort drinks, considering she was still reeling from her breakup a couple of months before. However, Katella offered to drive and said she didn't plan on drinking all that much, and before Harper was mentally ready for tonight, she found herself in the passenger seat of a sleek, black Mercedes-Benz.

Katella looked gorgeous. The Hanson sisters were known for both their brains and their beauty. Seraphina was more earthy, while Katella was more classic. Her strawberry blonde was swept up in a loose knot and her makeup was heavy without being overwhelming. She wore a ruched violet dress that was both short and low without being slutty. Her breasts were emphasized by the push-up bra, as were her long legs. In fact, if Harper had to guess, Katella knew exactly what to hide and what to show off. It was probably why the Gulls' Girls - the National Hockey League's version of cheerleaders that swept the ice during the breaks throughout the games - were voted as the top choice amongst fans last year. Katella was their coach, their coordinator, and their designer. She knew what worked and what didn't.

In fact, as much as people criticized Seraphina, Katella was ripped the first few months after her grandfather's murder. Not only had she not inherited the team even though she was older by a year, she was dating one of the players openly and proudly. She had a public breakup and was partly blamed for the Gulls' terrible season. She was labeled as a curse and questions swirled about what was wrong with her that not even her grandfather would trust her with his team.

To be honest, Harper hadn't been sure what to expect when it came to Katella. She was preparing for someone a little more forward, a little less tactful, but so far, Katella was sweet and genuine, nothing like the papers made her out to be.

"Thanks for doing this," Katella said, finally breaking the ice and glancing at Harper from the corner of her eye. "I'm not really much of a club person either. But I help coordinate social excursions and team bonding sessions that correlate with social perception rather than the team bonding excursions the coach plans and is reserved for strictly the team. It's almost a requirement I show up."

"You don't like clubs?" Harper asked, her voice hesitating only slightly.

She watched as Katella's lip curled up but she kept her eyes focused on the road ahead of her. "I know that people think I'm the party girl because I'm basically the Gulls' event coordinator," she said and then snorted. "It doesn't bother me, how people perceive me. But to answer your question, no, I'm not a fan. I don't really drink. But I love dancing."

Harper smiled. "I hate it," she said, feeling herself relax in her seat. "I feel super awkward."

Katella laughed, nodding. "So do I," she said, "but being awkward is kind of fun."

BY THE TIME they reached the club, Harper had a newfound

respect for Katella Hanson. And there was a good chance she might actually have fun tonight.

Taboo was a nightclub located in the heart of Costa Mesa's outdoor mall. It looked small on the outside but Harper was almost positive it would be much bigger and louder when they walked through. There was already a line waiting to get in even though it was just after ten, when the club opened. Harper didn't see any members of the team but she did notice some people in line shoot her and Katella dirty looks when they got to walk past the line and, after a quick search through their purses, allowed in without even paying the cover fee.

The music was loud and the dance floor was small. It was halfway filled already. The bar wrapped around the edge of the room, and the dance floor was dead center. Mainstream pop music remixed in with techno was currently thumping. Harper hated when they transformed a song she liked into something she didn't, but decided to ignore the music as best as she could for now. Instead, she followed Katella past the dance floor, past the bar, through a small doorway that led to a quieter room only VIPs had access to. There was still music – a different song but the same style – but it was emptier, and there was a private bar in the corner. It also wasn't standing room only. There were couches and comfortable chairs.

It was the first time Harper felt cool, which was dumb because Harper didn't care about being cool one way or the other. She was one of the least cool people she knew. But walking into the club in a tight dress and high heels next to Katella made her feel like a badass. It didn't hurt that the people waiting in line gave her dirty looks as they did so.

Once they were inside, the lights were dim except for mood lighting and strobe lights moving and flashing different colors in time with the beat. The dance floor was remarkably small filled with bodies pressing close together trying to dance. The bar was located in the back, closest to the elevated cup section of the club, which was packed with people trying to buy drinks.

Harper felt her heart seize with intimidation and she had to clutch her purse tighter to refrain from reaching up and putting her hands over her ears. She stayed close to Katella as she led the two to the VIP section of the club. They had to walk up a small flight of sleek back stairs that had no hand railings so Harper had to be careful in her heels to walk up them. There was a big bouncer in black clothes standing next to the stairs. He didn't even check Katella's id as she walked up the stairs. Maybe he would assist should someone need him to.

When they reached the top, the club suddenly turned into a lounge. Low red couches and chairs and sleek glass coffee tables. An even smaller dance floor that was only half-full. Girls dressed in even shorter dresses, younger than Harper was, dancing on laps and forcing smiles. The men watched with mild interest, more interested in conversations with each other rather than the girls. They're probably desensitized to it, honestly.

Katella made her way past three tables before reaching the back where half the hockey team sat in the corner. A few of them had girls with them but most did not. There were a few power players as well who lit up when they saw Katella. It might have been just Harper but a couple of them looked just as uncomfortable as she felt despite being in a profession that stigmatized them as mute, beautiful young women.

"Zach," Katella said. She didn't have to shout his name because the music wasn't as loud here. "This is Harper. She'll be doing the character piece on you Seraphina spoke to you about earlier."

His eyes picked up from his drink - a bottle of beer half drunk - and locked onto Harper. She felt her breath pause but she refused to look away from his penetrating stare.

"You were at the press conference," he said in a low tone. Somehow, Harper could hear his words even over the music. "I noticed you. You were the only person there in jeans."

Harper clenched her jaw to keep it from dropping. How did he know that? Did he really notice her among the crowd of people? And if so, how could he possibly notice that with everything going on? She had been watching him the whole time and it appeared as though he hadn't even looked her way. Maybe she was wrong. She wasn't sure how she felt about his unnoticed scrutiny, either. Perhaps it was a good thing, though. Maybe he employed that talent on the ice.

He took a sip of his beer, looking away. He had a strong jawline and high cheekbones. Masculine. He wasn't pretty but he was attractive in a rough sort of way. The only thing soft about him was his eyebrows, which arched naturally over his eyes. He had a very distinct look about him; it was hard to look away.

"I'm not really sure this is a good place to talk," he said, shifting his eyes back to her. "Do you want to go somewhere quieter?"

"I'm not going home with you!" She didn't know why she sounded so defensive. Even he seemed surprised by her outburst.

She pressed her lips together and looked away. How completely unprofessional. God, she had one chance to change the stereotype of particular female hockey fans where she genuinely cared about the sport and strategy rather than the attractiveness of the players and how to swindle them into marriage so her life would be set. The first words out of her mouth to Zachary Ryan was rejecting his possible advances. But the thing was, judging by the look on his face, that was not his intention. At all.

"Okay, well I'm glad we got that out of the way," he said. He tilted his head to the side and gave Harper a long look. "What would make you think you're my type anyway? You aren't married."

Harper instinctively curled the fingers of her left hand into a fist. He picked up on the fact that she wore no wedding ring. He was perceptive. More so than she could ever have expected.

"You don't mean that." She didn't know why she was

defending him from himself. Who was she? Some woman instructed to write about this player who broke contract and demanded to be traded after the Bangles booed him - their own player - when he came into the ice because rumor has it he slept with his teammate's wife. Harper didn't really care about the truth of it but now she was curious. Zach never publically commented but the team seemed to completely isolate him and the fans seemed to hate him. But that didn't make the rumors true.

"How do you know?" he asked, genuinely curious with a hint of a challenge in his tone. "You don't know me."

"No," Harper agreed with a smile, "but it's my job to find out who you are."

Zach rolled his eyes, causing Harper to frown.

"Everyone has their perception of me," he said before taking another swig of beer. "You heard the questions they threw at me. Not about my fifty-plus points, not about my sixty-seven percent win in the faceoff circle, not about my thirty plus goals per season in my eight-year career. It's about my personal life."

"Yeah, well, let's write a different story," Harper said. "I'm just trying to do my job and part of your job is dealing with the press. So." She grabbed a small notepad from her clutch. "Let's get started."

Chapter 4

THE NIGHT WAS MANAGEABLE. Harper wouldn't necessarily call it fun but it was definitely enlightening. Zachary Ryan was as arrogant as she initially believed and then some. He oozed confidence and had no problem talking about what he was good at. What Harper found she liked about him was that he had no problem admitting what he needed to work on. He didn't check out all the girls that were clamoring for attention or an autograph though he didn't completely ignore them either. He answered her questions without preamble, direct and to the point. She started getting a better understanding of who he was and she found that she began to respect him, despite the rumors.

Harper made sure she didn't touch on his personal life unless it directly correlated to the sport, such as who took him to hockey practice, when did he start playing, who were his childhood heroes he looked up to for motivation. She made no move to ask about girlfriends or his mysterious love life - he never seemed to have a steady girlfriend though there were a few casual ones - or even touch on the rumors that followed him from Toronto.

She and Katella ended up leaving relatively early - a few hours after they arrived - both seemingly content with their respective nights. Harper noticed Katella dancing a lot with Alexander Vane, the defensive player who was also a goon, poised to send a message or start a fight if the team needed it. Katella was a fabulous dancer and in Alexander's hands, she moved beautifully, liked she belonged there. As far as Harper saw, they didn't make out at any point but there was chemistry that was undeniable.

"Thanks again," Harper said when Katella took her to her car.

"Thank you," Katella said with a smile and a wave before heading inside. "Have fun at practice tomorrow."

That's right, Harper thought to herself. *I have another article I need to write.* She smirked to herself as she slid in the car. God, she loved her job.

⸻

HARPER FINISHED her article on Zack Ryan the next day. She emailed it to Seraphina and took her time to do what she always did on Sunday - walk the Back Bay and buy a frozen banana on Balboa Island. When she got home, Seraphina emailed her back with a couple of edits and the approval for it to be published on the Gulls' blog that day. It didn't take long for Harper to post it, and from there, she shut off her computer, refused to check her smartphone, and decided to play her game.

Monday morning, she received an eight AM call from Seraphina requesting she attend the Gulls' nine am practice and write a piece about how they look. "And be honest," Seraphina added. "Practices are open to the public so don't bullshit. Not that you ever do, but don't feel you need to write as a homer."

Harper hopped in the shower and threw on her clothes - a fitted plaid shirt with the long sleeves rolled up to the elbows, tight skinny jeans, and worn converse shoes. She didn't have time to blow dry her hair so she tossed the wet locks in a messy bun and threw an old baseball cap over it. A couple of stray strands slipped out of the binding and framed her face. She hoped they wouldn't frizz up when they dried.

The drive was easy - no more than fifteen minutes - but the parking wasn't as empty as she expected. A lot of people probably wanted to see the new team practice together. Once she parked, she grabbed her tote bag and headed into the arena. The practice rink was down a long circular hall and broke off to the right. She slipped in unnoticed and headed up the stairs where half the stone rows were already filled with spectators.

Harper took a seat off to the side just as the Zamboni finished cleaning the ice. She pulled out her notebook and pen, and once the players made their way into the ice, began to take notes.

———

THE TEAM WAS RUSTY. No doubt about it. There was no syncopation yet because the majority of them had never played together. However, they had potential. That much was clear.

Besides Ryan, there were nine new players Seraphina acquired either through waivers or during the off-season. NHL analysts actually gave the team an A+ for their acquisitions because Seraphina managed to increase depth while remaining well under cap. Some still criticized her choices - there were a few players with controversies of their own, including Alexander Vane, a fourth line goon who was arrested for battery after he defended a female fan from a groping male and Oscar Solis, a top defenseman known for being a pest on the blue line and who, like Zachary, had no problem answering the call to fight if need be. Gregory Russell was the person Seraphina spent the most money on but someone worthy of the investment, despite the fact that he was in his early thirties and kind of a jerk. He was a second line center with more experience than Zachary

Ryan, but no Cup. Kyle Underwood would serve as Ryan's right winger.

Harper was waiting outside the locker room for the team to get decent before she got to go in and interview them exclusively. Questions swirled in her mind and she kept clicking her pen, trying to make sure they made sense to her, trying to make sure she didn't sound like a complete fool when she interviewed these players, the coaches.

Someone propped the door open, indicating that she was free to come in. She took a breath and made sure her recorder was on and she was ready. When she stepped in, the first thing she noticed was the smell. It reeked of body odor and body spray and she had to hold her breath so she wouldn't choke. They were gathered in a circle around their coach, all of them listening to what he was saying. No one really noticed her, which she preferred so she could get ready and prepare. Everyone except Zachary Ryan, that is.

His crisp blue eyes found her and he gave her a little half smirk, like he could see straight through her. Like he knew she was frazzled on the inside despite the cool demeanor she was holding onto on the inside. His dark blond hair was messy and sweaty and the crease from his helmet was visible on his forehead. He had no shirt on - *oh my god, look at that body. Now I know how rappers feel when they talk about butts* - so his broad shoulders and toned chest and sculpted abdominal muscles glistened with sweat for everyone to see.

Well, actually, only for her to see since his teammates weren't exactly checking him out.

She gritted her teeth and forced herself to look away. She would not look at him. She would not let him get to her.

"...lot of work to do," Coach Cherney concluded. He clapped his hands together before rubbing them up and down. "But we can get through it. We've just gotta stick to the plan."

When he finished, Cherney looked over at Harper, as though he knew she had been there the entire time. "You're

Harper, right?" he asked. He waved her over before she could respond. "Sera told me about you. You're here to write about our practice."

Harper swallowed as every player turned to look at her. She refused to notice Zach's smile get bigger on his face.

She cleared her throat. "Um, yes." She nodded her head and felt her fingers clutch her pen tighter. She hated attention. She liked writing for a reason. It gave her the opportunity to work alone where she answered to no one but herself. Now, she was still writing - for a salary and health benefits - but she was given assignments that involved her interviewing people and spending time with them and getting to know them. And not just a few people, but an entire hockey team and their coaching staff.

"Why don't you introduce yourself to us, and then you can grab a few players and get some quotes," Cherney suggested.

Cherney was intimidating even though he was a smaller-built guy. When he played hockey, he used to play defense, which didn't make sense because he was so small and so lean. He was bald with a bushy mustache that crawled over his top lip. He was known for being direct and had no problem being confrontational. He was old school and did things his way without adapting to the times, which could definitely be an issue depending on how this new team responded to his coaching. However, he seemed to be nothing short of friendly and Seraphina had nothing but good things to say about him. Even now, he was looking at her with warmth even though they had yet to be formally introduced.

Except for the fact that he was making her introduce herself to everyone. Except for the fact that he put her on the spot.

"I'm Harper," she said, forcing a smile. She sounded more confident than she felt, which was a good thing. She hoped her smile came off as genuine rather than as a grimace. "You'll be seeing a lot of me. I'm the team blogger and I'll be writing a lot about you as players, you as people, and you as a team. If you have any questions, feel free to reach out to me."

"Do you let your subjects read the articles you write before you publish them?"

Harper's eyes narrowed in on Zach. There was that dry glint in his eye, the cocky smirk on his chiseled face. He stood there without a shirt on, only in the leggings all hockey players wore under their hockey pants, padding, and socks. She refused to look at his chest, refused to explore the muscles with her eyes, refused to give him that satisfaction. He was a gorgeous specimen but he knew that and it took any endearment away.

"Are you worried?" The quip was out of her mouth before she could stop it and her tone was challenging and possibly flirtatious.

Especially after her conversation from last night.

She didn't like the way he was looking at her. She didn't like that gleam in his eyes, the particular curve of his smile directed at her, his body language. But she was starting to understand who he was and she knew how to respond to that. She wasn't nervous around him anymore. In fact, she was secure, bold in her confidence of herself. He liked a challenge; she would give it to him.

"If you have any questions," she said, her eyes finding Zach once again. "I have an office on the second floor of the Ice Palace that I will be moving into Monday. Feel free to reach out to me. I look forward to working with you."

The team collectively welcomed her in their own way but she didn't hear them. He hadn't looked away from her. Another challenge. She got that.

Challenge accepted.

God, she hoped it wasn't flirtatious.

Chapter 5

HARPER SENT both of her articles to Seraphina late Sunday night. Besides a couple of tweaks, the articles were published exactly as they were on the website late Monday night. She even had a couple of complimentary comments left the last time she checked. This was gelling and it felt good. She couldn't wait to bring it up to her grandmother when she checked in on her.

"So," Terrie Immings said, sitting across from Harper at her round kitchen table, her long fingers - fingers that used to play that old piano in the living room beautifully - tapping the surface. "How does the team look? I heard we got Zachary Ryan. How's he?"

Harper shrugged, swallowing a mouthful of fresh lemonade. It was Tuesday, early afternoon, and the sun was seeping through the open kitchen window, making the kitchen look both lighter and bigger than it really was.

"I haven't really seen him play, Grandma," Harper said once her mouth was clear. "But he'll be first line center, so he must be good. Cherney wouldn't put him there unless he wasn't."

Terrie snorted, rolling her blue eyes. "He was out there because Matt Peters left," she said. "He had a shitty season, let

28

me tell you. I'm not sure if it was because of his relationship with Katella, or if it's because he had already mentally checked out after Brown's death. Regardless, he was lucky to play for us and he gave us a half-assed season. I'm hoping Ryan turns it all around for us."

"Well, the guy has scored thirty goals since his rookie season," Harper pointed out. "That's eight seasons with thirty goals per season. Plus, the last four years, he's had fifty plus assists. He's a sixty percent average in the faceoff circle, which can be improved upon but is still really impressive, and last year, he was ranked a plus thirteen even though the Bangles didn't make the playoffs. He wasn't even first line with them."

"What is it, Harp?" she asked. "You sound skeptical."

Harper pressed her lips together, trying to think of the right thing to say. She knew how to write down her thoughts, no problem, but to organize her thoughts in a way where she could communicate them verbally... That was an entirely different story.

"On paper, he looks perfect," Harper said. "Besides his off-ice issues, the only problem I see is his attitude. He's top line material but he has over a hundred penalty minutes his last three seasons. He's a skilled player but he'll fight - which is respectable, but then he broke his hand during a fight and was out of the lineup for thirty games."

"And he still managed to score thirty goals?" Terrie pointed out, though she legitimately sounded intrigued.

"He doesn't wear a shield either," Harper added, "which, I know since the National Hockey League's shield regulations were grandfathered in, he doesn't have to, but it screams reckless, arrogant behavior."

Terrie smirked. "Sounds like my kind of player," she said.

Harper rolled her eyes but a good-natured smile tugged at her lips. Her grandmother was a character, there was no denying that. She had been prim and proper, the perfect defini-tion of a nineteen fifties housewife. It wasn't until her children were out of the house did she start smoking cigars during the Stanley Cup playoffs and swearing when she was driving. Her personality began to emerge during the acquisition of more independence. When her husband died, she allowed herself two weeks to mourn the love of her life before she decided life was too short and threw herself into her passions.

"You should come with me to the practice," Harper said, teasing her grandmother with a wink. "I get to go into the locker rooms afterward and interview them without their shirts."

"You're getting paid to talk to naked men?" Terrie asked, her brow pushed up under her hairline. Her pale green eyes were clearly impressed. "Honey, I would have killed for your job."

Harper laughed. She loved spending time with her grandmother. It didn't even feel like a burden to take care of her by any means. In fact, Harper aspired to be more like her grandmother. She loved life and had no problem expressing who she was. She didn't care how people perceived her or what they said about her. She was who she was and was unapologetic about it. Harper was relatively the same except she did worry about what people thought about her. Which was stupid. Which was why she spent as much of her free time as she could with her.

"Go home, Harper," she said with a smile. "I can get myself into bed. You have a busy day tomorrow. Charity function, right? Do you have a dress? Let me give you some money to get a dress. Get a slutty one. You have a great set of tits, Harper. Use them to your advantage."

Harper started laughing. "My advantage?" she asked. "What am I using my boobs for?"

"You're going to marry a hockey player," she said as though it were the most obvious thing in the world. "You've got to catch their attention with your looks and make them fall in love with your personality."

Harper rolled her eyes but a smile still permeated her face. "Grams, you have quite an imagination," she said as she stood up and collected her keys.

30

"Of course I do," her grandmother replied. "Why else do you think your grandfather was so satisfied in life?"

———

IT WAS dark by the time Harper returned to her apartment. The days were getting shorter with October fast approaching and there was a chill in the air that hadn't been there before. Harper didn't mind; she loved the cold.

She changed into a long sleeved thermal and blue plaid pajama bottoms, leaving her socks on and her hair down. She was just about to remove her bra and settle into bed with a good book when a knock interrupted her. She pressed her brows together. No one visited her after six at night. She only had a couple of friends who would stop by and they would only let her know ahead of time. Her only family was her grandmother and she didn't drive and she definitely wasn't dating anyone, which just begged the question - who was at the door?

She padded over the carpet living room to her door and rolled up to her toes to check out her peephole. Her heart skipped to her throat.

What the hell was Bryan doing on her doorstep?

She hesitated. Her teeth started gnawing the inside of her bottom lip. She didn't want to answer. She was compelled not to. They had a bad breakup several months ago and he was the last person she ever wanted to see again. That was why she broke up with him. Because he was a terrible, controlling person that teetered onto mental abuse. She spent a year and a half with the guy; she didn't want to spend another minute of it with him again.

"Harp?" he called, knocking on the door. "Come on, open the door. I know you're there."

Her heart seized up and skipped a beat. She hated his voice; it grated on her the way fingernails dragging on chalkboard did. She pressed her back against the door as gently as she could, keeping her position crouched, preventing herself from being seen. As if Bryan could see her through the peephole. She held her breath, willing him to go away. She wanted him to go away.

Her phone started vibrating against the wooden television stand. It sounded like a car horn on an empty street. It made her jump and nearly lose her balance.

"Come on, I can hear your phone. I know you don't go anywhere without your phone."

Harper pressed her hands against her mouth, ensuring she didn't make any telling noise. She didn't care if he thought she was gone. All she cared about was getting him off her doorstep. She had no idea why he was here. It wasn't like he had any of her stuff and she definitely didn't have any of his. There was no reason for him to be here. She didn't want him to be here.

Her phone stopped vibrating. The light went off. She held her breath, waiting. Waiting.

Then: "I just wanted to congratulate you on your position with the Gulls. I know how much you love hockey and you're such a talented writer, you completely deserve it. Your article on Zachary Ryan was superb. Great job. I look forward to your next one. That's it. That's all I wanted to say."

More silence. Then footsteps walking away.

She let out a sigh of relief. She could finally catch her breath. The tension still hadn't left her body. It probably wouldn't until she was tucked into bed and Bryan was far from her mind. Far, but not forgotten.

Harper hated her body's reaction whenever Bryan was involved, even if one of her friends brought him up casually, even if her grandmother made a disparaging comment about him in an off-handed way. Her palms would start to sweat, her stomach would clench up, and her entire body would completely freeze. Her heartbeat would start to get harder and faster and she could feel her pulse gently slice a corner in her neck. She felt out of control, losing her grip, and she had no idea how to calm herself down. Her instinct was to curl up in a ball and shelter herself from the outside world until Bryan was gone from her mind and she could breathe again.

She didn't love him anymore but she wasn't over him. He still controlled her in this way and she wanted to end it, she wanted to get her life back so if she saw him on the street, she could walk past him with her shoulders back, her head held high, and not even blink.

Harper let out a shaky breath and forced herself to stand. She wanted to change this about herself. She didn't know how to overcome this but she would. Somehow. Especially with Bryan knowing where she lived and forcing his way back into her life.

For now, she would focus on her new job. Hockey. Her grandmother. Bryan wouldn't even enter her thoughts at all.

Before she went to her bedroom, Harper checked the door and the windows one last time to ensure Bryan couldn't get to her in any way possible.

Chapter 6

IT WAS a few more weeks of practices and blog posts about how the team was slowly coming together and becoming one cohesive unit until the first exhibition game at the Sea Side Ice Palace. These games were fun and interactive with the fans where many of the skilled players would work in various jobs throughout the Palace in order to act on a more personal level with the fans. This way, the rookies and new players had a chance to play NHL hockey as well as show off their skill in hopes to make the team. A lot of fans paid decent money to attend these games in order to see their favorite players play but there was risk in putting top players in practice games - injury and fights sometimes broke out among especially competitive rookies vying for roster spots who wanted to prove just how dedicated they were by going after skilled players. As such, many teams throughout the NHL chose to sit their top players for a couple of exhibition games intermittently.

Harper was actually looking forward to the game. Seraphina offered her and her grandmother tickets in their two-hundred level suite - the closest suites to the glass on the first level of the Palace, but Harper politely declined. She preferred being up close and personal and when Seraphina found out, she forced Harper to take two glass seats at center ice with unlimited access to the different food vendors the Ice Palace hosted.

When Harper told her grandmother, Terrie Immings let out a whoop of excitement and asked if there were any part time jobs available for her, mentioning things like towel girl, water girl, or locker room girl. What locker room girl was, Harper did not want to know.

Bryan had not made another impromptu appearance at her home, something Harper was grateful for. In fact, she had reached a point where every little noise did not cause her to immediately look to the door, flinching as she did so. She shouldn't be uncomfortable or feel unsafe in her own home and she hated that she was. Maybe she should heed her grandmother's advice and seek a psychologist, something to try not to be afraid of him. Her fear only gave him power and she did not want to do that anymore. She already wasted a year and a half of being with him and a year being without him. She was ready to move on.

Which was probably why she threw herself into her writing. For the most part, Harper wrote her blogs in her office. They typically took her thirty to sixty minutes and another hour for editing and uploading. She had to justify the next six hours of remaining time in her office so she started listening to audiobooks and working out. When Seraphina found out, she had cardio machines delivered to her office, no questions asked.

The players rarely stopped by even though she stayed on the off-chance they wanted to discuss anything with her. She always made sure to let them know her door was always open, especially if they had a story idea to pitch. She wrote almost daily but her most popular article was on Zachary Ryan. She had over three hundred comments and counting. Because she kept up with them when they first began, it was easy to maintain a discussion with anyone who posed questions or had differing opinions or points to make.

Now, if she wanted to keep writing, she couldn't answer everyone, especially when half of them were puck princesses asking for details about Zachary Ryan's love life. Harper couldn't help but roll her eyes but at the same time, she understood the curiosity. Were the rumors true? Had he slept with his teammate's wife? Was that why Toronto was so quick to get rid of him? They were questions she wanted to ask, questions she knew were none of her business.

The game wasn't crowded at all and Seraphina kept her promise by getting glass seats for she and her grandmother. The seats were just right of center, close to where the net the Gulls would defend twice. When the puck was on the opposite side of the ice, they would have to lean forward in order to see but because there was nothing in their way inhibiting them, that wasn't be too much of a problem. They got there a half hour before the game because Terrie liked to watch them warm up, hooting and hollering in her blue and white striped Gulls beanie. If Harper was being honest, she thought her grandmother might be a bigger fan than she was, which was saying a lot.

"What number is Zachary Ryan?" she asked her granddaughter, leaning closer to Harper but mewing her eyes on the players.

"15," Harper said. "His number in Toronto was 51 but because that was Stevenson's before he retired, he decided to invert the numbers out of respect."

"But they didn't retire Stevenson's number," Terrie said, quirking a brow. "He didn't have to give up his number?"

Harper shook her head. "As far as I know, no," she said.

The warmup was typical - the players skated around their half of the ice, stretching, stick handling, warming up. A few were known to interact with fans, dispensing picks to kids with big posters showing love to their favorite players. Most of the girls were dressed accordingly for the cold environment but there were a few with short skirts and tank tops, trying to get the attention of at least one of the players. Harper was pleased to see they were all focused on their game and not looking for any distraction. Hopefully, that focus translated into a good game.

Surprisingly enough, the majority of the skilled players were on the ice while the majority of the prospects and rookies were working in the food stands or at the club level of the Ice Palace. Traditionally, exhibition games allowed the rookies and prospects to show off their skill, give them a chance to play national level hockey as well as allow them to try out for the team. If Harper had to speculate, Cherney wanted to give his players as many opportunities to develop chemistry as possible before the season began. As long as his players weren't over-worked, it was a good strategy.

"How do you think we're going to do?" Terrie asked after the national anthem. She had to shout over the music, the announcer outlining the game and the opponents. When Harper shrugged, she elbowed her granddaughter. "You've been watching them practice, girl. I want your professional take!"

"Honestly," Harper said, turning from the ice so she could look at her grandmother, "I think it could go either way. The talent is there, they just have to find the chemistry and they're not going to do that in practice. I mean, it's built there, of course. But a game and practice are two separate beasts, and chemistry, for the most part, doesn't happen overnight." She shrugged her shoulders. "That's my professional take on it."

"We have a lot of players," Terrie pointed out.

"We do," Harper acknowledged with a nod. "Absolutely we do. But those players are good individually, although I suppose you could argue Ryan got his stats from his passing and you need wingers to receive a pass in order to get those stats. But we need the players to be good together. We need a good team rather than simply have a bunch of good players. I also think Cherney is one hell of a coach, so if anyone can get this team to where it could be, it's him."

The large overhead big screen television had a clock

counting down until zero - the start of the game. The two linesmen and the two referees (differentiated by an orange armband) skated out at the two-minute mark. Even though it was the first practice game, some of the spectators still booed, due to the antagonistic relationship the Gulls had had with the refs. Because they had been a chippy team - and especially with the addition of Alexander Vane - they had a reputation they couldn't defend nor could they change. As such, calls tended to go against them or legitimate penalties on them weren't called at all. After the refs, the challenging team, the San Francisco Prisoners, skated out to louder boos. Finally, the lights got dark and the announcer enthusiastically announced the Gulls. Harper and her grandmother got to their feet, clapping and cheering.

After circling their half of the ice, the only players that didn't go to the bench was the starting line - consisting of center Zachary Ryan, left winger Kyle Underwood, and right winger Alec Schumacher. The two defensive players were rookie eighteen-year-old Erik Karlsson and twenty-four-year old Edward Sheen. Finally, the goalie was Brandon Thorpe, captain of the team and Vezina nominee last year, despite their lackluster season.

"Must be their first line," Harper murmured to herself. Which would make sense since the Prisoners were one of the Gulls' rivals.

Because the Gulls' were home, Cherney had the opportunity to switch his lines up right before the refs blew the whistle to start the game after any breakages. If this was the first line, it would follow that the Prisoners' first line was also out, but unlike the Gulls', the majority of their veteran players were sitting this game out. They were probably up in the media booth, donning suits and watching from there.

The game wasn't as fast paced as hockey games usually tended to be. There was chemistry between Zach and Kyle, which was both surprising and not - both were extremely talented players and putting them together seemed to be the logical choice, one any coach would have made in Cherney's position. However, what was surprising was the way the two immediately clicked, like they were brothers from different wombs.

Kyle was one of the few players still on the team that came from Henry Wayne's era. Harper didn't know much about him other than the fact that he was a consistent, thirty goals a season player who dated Emma Winsor, a recent UCI grad who majored in dance. He was a quiet player. Kyle did have an antagonistic reputation, however. She knew if he was on any other team, she would absolutely detest him. He was gritty and wasn't afraid to get on the crease to catch a rebound or get a dirty goal. He was also one of the few skilled players who wasn't afraid to respond to a challenge if someone wanted to fight. Unless, of course, the other team was purposefully trying to get him off the ice.

It was a surprisingly chippy first period. A lot of the prospects were trying to earn their stripes, stepping up to defend the skilled players when they took offense to a late hit or a snide remark. They wanted to do everything they could to guarantee them a roster spot. The majority of the prospects would be sent down to the minor league, which was conveniently located in San Diego, but there were a few standout players that Harper knew Cherney had his eye on, including a nineteen-year old goal tender they signed last year. He was regarded as a steal during the second round during the draft. In fact, there were whispers that the kid - an American by the name of Jimmy Stafford - could replace Brandon Thorpe as starting goalie in as little as two years, depending on the conditioning he received. Harper thought that was a little too presumptuous right now since he still had yet to play his first NHL game but he was definitely one of those players to keep an eye on.

The rest of the game was much like the first period - quick and chippy. Thorpe started the game but, for some reason, was giving up soft goals - goals he, as a professional NHL goaltender, should have had no problem stopping. Like all exhibition games, it was high scoring and not as intense as it would have been during the season. But it was still exciting to watch.

Harper was pleased to see that Zachary Ryan's reputation preceded him. He was an excellent center, winning fifty-four percent of his faceoffs, making key, crisp passes, and possessing one of the strongest shots on the team - when he used it. That was his biggest problems - the fact that he didn't shoot as much as he should have, especially since he had a few opportunities where he probably would have scored. Instead, he chose to pass. But it was something that could be improved.

The Gulls lost their first exhibition game by a goal - four to five. But they were a much better team than last year's Gulls had ever been.

There was hope. That was all that mattered.

Chapter 7

IT WAS JUST AFTER MIDNIGHT, a couple hours after the game ended, when Harper's cell phone started blasting Miranda Lambert. She cracked open one eye and glared as best as she could. It wasn't a number she had in her cell phone but the 949 area code immediately ruled out Bryan so she answered it, just in case it had to do with her grandmother.

"Hello?" Her voice came out groggy and incomprehensible.

"Harper?" a familiar voice responded, loud and full of life. There was noise in the background that made the caller shout. "Is that you? Are you there? It's Kat. Katella, from work."

"Oh." Harper felt herself relax, knowing that her grandmother was okay. She sat in bed and leaned back against the wall, stifling a yawn as best as she could. "Hi. What's up?"

"Were you sleeping?" Katella asked on the other end. "Oh my God, Harper I am so sorry! I didn't mean to wake you. I just, I'm a little drunk and I needed to talk to someone and I didn't know who else to call. I can't talk to Seraphina about it because she's the cause but, um..." She let her voice trail off and Harper couldn't help but musing that for someone who was tipsy, she didn't slur her words very much. "I guess I just needed someone. But I'll let you go. I'm sorry, I'm being selfish and totally not the twenty-seven-year old I'm supposed to be."

"No, no." Harper rubbed her face with her palm, trying to wake herself up. "It's fine. What's up?"

"Did you hear about Peters training with us?" she asked. Her voice had a slight screech to it but that was probably the alcohol. "Yeah, no one picked up his sorry ass when he was a free agent before the trade deadline and now he's going to condition with the team and try and make it with us again. That fucker. His flight came in just before the game and he had the audacity to grab a last minute ticket. Can you believe him?"

Harper had to press her lips together to keep from laughing. The situation wasn't funny, of course, but Katella seemed to be a funny albeit slightly dramatic drunk, which was incredibly amusing.

"How can I help you?" Harper asked because, really, she had no idea what to say.

"Well, um..." Katella let her voice trail off and Harper was ready to throw her phone across the room. She had always been particular about her sleep; in all honesty, she had no idea how people were able to stay up late and wake up early. Sleep was an integral part of her routine and as much as she cared about Katella, Katella was interrupting that routine. "Can you come get me? I came here with Vane but I don't want to make him leave and I definitely don't want him to know I'm leaving because I don't want to deal with Peters, you know? I would call Seraphina but I know she has an early morning and I'm sure you do too and I'm so sorry but... I just didn't know who else to call."

Harper felt her stomach clench. "You're at Taboo?" she asked, running her fingers through her hair.

There was a muffled sound, and somehow, Harper knew Katella was nodding. "Oh," she said, her words slurred. "You can't see me. Yes, I'm here. I think I want to go home. I don't think I want to do this anymore, Harper. Can you help me?"

Harper shook her head to herself, inhaling sharply as silently as she could. "As best as I can," she said. "I'll be there in twenty minutes."

Katella started gushing about how nice and sweet Harper was but Harper hung up, deciding she wouldn't know the difference. She forced herself out of bed and grabbed a shirt off of her desk chair - a plaid shirt that brought out the green in her eyes - and a pair of jeans from the floor. She threw on a jacket and a pair of old sneakers and instead of brushing her hair, she chose to tie it up into a messy bun instead. She left without even putting on makeup because her intention was definitely not to stay. She wanted to be back in bed as fast as she could.

The drive to Taboo was quick and easy. Since it was so late, she got there in less than ten minutes. Parking took her another five minutes but she managed to find a spot close to the entrance so she wouldn't have to worry about being a female walking around by herself in the middle of the night outside a nightclub. Surprisingly enough, there wasn't that much of a line and the bouncer must have recognized her from before because he waved her right in without making her pay a cover fee or giving her a hard time about her attire.

It was a tad more intimidating to enter a nightclub by herself but she swallowed her fear and tilted her chin up, completely ignoring the club's patrons giving her amused looks due to her attire. Perhaps she should have thrown on a dress and a cute pair of flats. It definitely would have made her feel more comfortable.

Harper decided she would head to the VIP section from before in hopes that that was where she would find Katella. When she saw the familiar head of blonde hair, a sweep of relief pushed through her body, only to be eliminated when she realized half the team was here as well.

"Shit," she muttered to herself.

"Harper!" a drunk enough Katella exclaimed, dashing over to her in high heels and somehow not toppling over due to her clear inebriation. Katella had a talent some women would kill for. "You came!"

When she reached Harper, she threw her arms around her and pulled her close. Harper could smell the strong scent of expensive alcohol permeating her breath, along with something artificially sweet. She felt completely awkward, standing next to Katella - who, besides a pair of heels, wore a mini dress and professional makeup - made her feel like an ugly duckling. Not in the sense that she lacked confidence in her looks, only that Harper felt out of place and insecure about how she appeared right now.

"Are you ready to go?" Harper asked. She hoped the edge in her voice was only something she could hear because she didn't want to come off as demanding but her exhaustion was hitting her now and she wanted nothing better than to rid herself of the clothes she wore so she could crawl back into bed for some sleep.

"Already?" Katella asked, pulling away from her and looking down at her with her big, sea-green eyes. Both she and Seraphina had green eyes, but Seraphina's resembled Christmas trees while Katella's resembled the ocean. "But you just got here. Can we stay a few more minutes? Please?" She sounded like a child, which annoyed Harper but she didn't want to deal with it.

She nodded but said nothing, causing Katella to clap and find Alexander Vane once more. Harper allowed herself to finally roll her eyes. She wasn't sure what she should do now. Waiting seemed like the most logical thing but her presence was already awkward and somewhat standoffish. She didn't want to damper the atmosphere even more than she had. She was obviously a designated driver and not someone who came to dance and party and, judging by the fact that ever other moment was a yawn, she didn't particularly want to be here.

"You look nice," a voice said. The only reason Harper even knew he was talking to her was because he placed a hand on the small of her back and when she jumped at the contact, he chuckled. "Clearly you came prepared and ready to party."

Harper turned and found Zach's sky blue eyes staring at her, his lips cocked into an amused smirk. He wore a simple white v-neck and dark blue jeans. He looked really, really good. She bit her bottom lip to keep from saying something dumb or making a noise or emphasizing the awkwardness.

"Um, yeah, hi," she said. Internally, she shook her head and felt her face heat up. She sounded like such a loon.

"So," he said, sliding his hands into his pockets and rolling his shoulders back. "I never took you for a plaid girl. It suits you."

She laughed, despite herself. "Thanks?" she asked with a grin. She looked around; a slight awkwardness touched their conversation and she crossed her arms over her chest and placed her eyes back on Zach. "So, is this your thing?"

He leaned in closer so he could hear her. "My thing?" he asked, perking a brow.

"Your scene," she explained. "Is this what you like to do? Come to clubs and drink and socialize?"

He shrugged. "Going out with the guys after a game makes for good bonding," he explained. "I don't know if I would call it my thing but I like the atmosphere. I like how laid back everyone is. I like drinking socially and meeting new people. It's nice." Harper snorted before she could stop herself and he shot her a look. "Let me guess - you're one of those girls who thinks clubs are silly and a waste of time and sexist because you have scantily dressed girls grinding on guys who want nothing more than to have sex and get free drinks?" He rolled his eyes. "It's a quid pro quo relationship. Girls get to feel attractive, guys get to feel powerful. I don't think there's" -

"You really don't think, do you?" Harper asked, tilting her head to the side.

"What are you talking about?" he asked.

"I don't care if this is your scene," Harper said honestly. "I don't care what people do to bring them joy. It doesn't affect me so there's no reason for me to judge them. I was just trying to make conversation."

He pressed his lips together, his brow pushed up so high it crawled up to his hairline. "Oh."

"You're kind of defensive, aren't you?" she asked.

"I..." He reached up to cup the back of his neck with his palm, glancing away. "I'm just so used to people trying to tell me what I should and shouldn't do, what's right, what's wrong. No one is just happy with me as me, you know? So I apologize for taking that out on you."

Harper gave him an odd look. "There's no reason to apologize," she told him before narrowing her eyes. "You never answered my question."

"About?"

"Whether or not you liked this sort of place," she said.

His smirk grew into a full-fledged smile. "Dance with me," he said, taking her hand in his and tugging her to the dance floor.

Harper was surprised that she put up no resistance. She really must be tired.

Chapter 8

HARPER STILL COULD NOT BELIEVE Zach managed to talk her into dancing with her. Yes, Katella was busy making out with Alexander Vane on the dance floor to even remember Harper had shown up - in jeans and a plaid shirt, no less - and Zachary Ryan was pulling her onto the dance floor and the crazy part about this was, she wasn't resisting. She was woken up not even an hour ago, threw on the first clothes she could find, and was out the door in less than fifteen minutes. She was exhausted, and the whole way over, all she could think about was crawling back into bed. But Zach was making her forget all that.

"I'm a terrible dancer," she made sure to tell him, shouting over the music.

"Who is actually a good dancer?" he replied with that half-smile, half-smirk. "All you need to do is pretend you're having sex." He furrowed his brow. "You have had sex before, haven't you?"

Harper felt her face heat up but even with her muddled, sleep-interrupted brain, she was quick to respond with, "My sex life is none of your business."

His smirk also turned into a full-fledged one.

"Also," she continued, once they were on the floor. "I don't particularly want to pretend to have sex with you."

"You'd rather really do it?" he teased. His blue eyes sparkled.

Harper felt herself ease, even when he placed his hands on her hips and pull her close to him so only centimeters filled space between them. She should have felt out of place with how she was dressed and the fact that her hair was thrown up into a bun and sneakers on her feet. The only reason she was able to get past the bouncers was because they recognized her from before. They didn't even care she wasn't following their strict dress code. It was nice having friends in high places. Yet being with Zach, having all of his attention focused solely on her, made her feel comfortable. Made her not even care a little bit that she looked like a slob in a sea full of masterpieces. He made her feel special and worthy and beautiful while simultaneously pushing her buttons and causing a reaction.

"You aren't dancing," he pointed out.

"Neither are you."

He smirked. Again. "Let's do it together, then," she said. "On the count of three. One... Two... Three."

And then they were moving and Harper was smiling and without even thinking about it, her hands found his shoulders - pure muscle and bone and two feet wide - and she found herself having fun. The music was a song she had never even heard of but that didn't particularly matter. Her hips found the beat and she started moving them as best as she could. It felt stiff and unnatural but she kept pushing through it until it felt easier and not as mechanical.

She looked up at him, finding his eyes on her. They weren't teasing or amused, just studious. She wasn't sure what he was looking at; her shirt was tight but there was definitely no cleavage showing, which meant he must be looking at her throat, her neck. Up until his eyes found hers and they just stared.

He looked at her like an archeologist looked at a historical artifact, like a collector looked at a first edition, like a hockey player looked at the Stanley Cup. In all honesty, she had no idea why he was looking at her but she found she liked it. Bryan had never looked at her that way and neither had previous boyfriends. To be honest, she didn't know men really looked at women this way, originally thinking it was just another phony component added to romance in television and books to cause impossible expectations in partners. Yet here Zach was, giving her a similar look, and they hadn't even kissed. They hadn't even dated.

"I like the color of your eyes," he said over the music. "I've never seen a green like yours before."

Harper hadn't expected a compliment, especially not from Zachary Ryan. He came off cocky and arrogant, potentially charming and standoffish. Not nice. Not sweet.

She wasn't quite sure how to react so she spun around, flipping her hair over her shoulder so it would cover the redness currently invading her cheeks. She shouted a quick thanks, though, for a minute, she considered pretending she hadn't heard him. That wouldn't have worked, however. Not when she was looking into his eyes when he said so.

She kept moving her hips to the music. She felt less stupid now that she realized no one but Zach was looking at her. In fact, dare she say she felt comfortable? Without warning, his hands found a place on her hips. She didn't jump at the unexpected touch. She didn't even tense up. He pushed her hips back and forth, controlling her pace, and she felt her lips curl up into a grin. She liked this. This was actually fun. His head came down by her face and the tip of his chin practically grazed her shoulder. She didn't know why but she was compelled to reach up with her right arm and throw it awkwardly around his neck, pulling him even closer to her. It was a bold move but it didn't mean anything significant. They were just having fun.

A holler pierced the air and Harper realized Katella and

Vane were dancing nearby. Katella, as tipsy as she was, knew how to keep in time with the music, no problem. She gave Harper an air high five and then a thumbs up. Harper couldn't help but laugh and shake her head.

"What's this?" Zach asked, his voice tickling her ear. She lost a grip on her breathing and she held what little breath she had in her throat as his low, soft voice invaded her space in the best kind of way. "Are you actually having fun?"

She laughed. "Yeah." She nodded and wasn't even ashamed or too stubborn to admit it. Because she was.

His grip tightened on her waist and he pulled her even closer to him, which she didn't mind. Which she found she liked. His hands managed to find a sliver of flesh - the in-between from her jeans and her shirt - and he placed his palms flat on that flesh and her insides jumped to attention under his touch. She liked when he touched her. She wondered if he felt anything when he touched her.

Her fingers started playing with his hair, his head turned a fraction so his lips were pressed to the column of her throat, her eyes rolled back and she pushed back against him -

"What the fuck are you doing?"

Harper's eyes sprung open and her body immediately filled with tension. She knew that voice. Somehow, her eyes found the voice immediately. She didn't even have to look for him to verify it.

There was Bryan, standing in a collared shirt and blue jeans. She had no idea why he was here. He never seemed interested in nightclubs when they were together but maybe that was because they were together. Maybe because she never seemed interested. His blond hair was spiked with gel casually, his blue eyes narrowed, his strong jaw locked in on Zach's hands on her stomach.

Harper didn't know if it was because he could feel her body completely shift but Zach stopped dancing the minute she did, and his hands stayed on her hips, holding onto her tightly, protectively.

"Do you know this guy?" Zach asked Harper, his eyes on her profile, completely ignoring Bryan.

"That's my girlfriend you have your hands all over, Ryan," Bryan said. He took a step toward the pair. "What - none of your new teammates have any girlfriends or wives for you to sleep with so you decide to go the administrative route?"

Zach immediately released Harper and went to step in front of her. "You want to repeat that?" he asked.

Harper went back to stand between them. "Ex girlfriend," she all but shouted, throwing a glare at Bryan as they did so. "For several months now."

"What are you doing with Zachary Ryan?" he asked her. He was maybe an inch shorter than Zach and leaner rather than bulky but Bryan was fit and fast. "You wrote one article about the guy and now you're at a nightclub, letting him put his hands all over you. I know you're a Gulls' fan, but Jesus Christ, I didn't realize you were a puck slut."

Without warning, Zach grabbed the collar of Bryan's shirt and pulled him close to him, taking advantage of that one-inch height discrepancy by looking down at Bryan over his nose.

"Do it," Bryan said. His voice was low and the music was loud but Harper could hear him clearly. She could see his lips, could read them like a book. Bryan's eyes were on Zach and Zach alone, something Harper was thankful for. She didn't want to admit it, but she knew if he looked at her, she would flinch away. And he would love that. "Punch me. Beat the shit out of me. See what happens."

Harper held her breath. She knew Zach wanted to do it. She didn't have to know him well to see that his anger and frustration was written plain as day on his face. In fact, his crystal blue eyes were dancing with furious flames that caused the irises to sharpen. His knuckles were white as he gripped Bryan's shirt tight and even though Harper knew he had a good hold on Bryan, that Bryan wasn't too heavy for him, Zach's hands still shook with pent up rage. She wasn't sure if it was because of her or if it was because of the blatant disrespect Bryan had for him. Either way, it was enough to provoke Zach into starting something with him, which might have been exactly what Bryan wanted. She knew she had to do something lest Zach actually do something he would later regret. Sure, he might not regret the action but he would regret the consequences. There was no reason for it to turn ugly and possibly risk Zach's career. Not only that, but he needed his hands to play hockey and she couldn't let him risk his career over Bryan. Bryan was nowhere near as important as that.

"Hey." Harper placed her hand on Zach's arm - she couldn't help but notice the bulge of his bicep stretch out the sleeve of his shirt, and how rock-hard it felt underneath her touch - and gently squeezed, hoping to get his attention. People were starting to look and whisper. It would be worse if they started pulling out their phones and taking pictures. God forbid a video of Zach beating Bryan up go viral. "Hey. It's okay. Let's go."

"It is not okay," Zach said, keeping his eyes on Bryan. His grip did not loosen. "He is not allowed to talk to you like that, especially in front of me."

"What, you think you're her boyfriend now?" Bryan asked with a sneer.

Zach growled and Harper immediately squeezed his arm tighter. "Zach, let's go," she said. "He's not worth it. He's not worth it." She didn't seem to be getting through to him; she had to up her game. As such, she stood on her toes and leaned toward his ear and whispered, "Please. Take me home."

She could see the minute he broke. Without warning, he dropped Bryan to the floor. "If I ever see you around her again without her permission, I'll make you regret the day you met her," he said. He threw his eyes at Harper, still angry, still burning. "Find Katella and Xander. We're going."

Harper swallowed and nodded. She didn't even notice Bryan slink out of the club.

Chapter 9

"YOU REALLY DON'T HAVE to do this," Harper said as she walked out with Zach on one side and Katella and Xander on the other. For an inebriated person, she walked skillfully in her heels and managed to maintain a sense of class. Lex seemed completely enamored with her, which made the romantic in Harper scream.

"Of course we do," Xander said on the other side of Katella. "You're one of us."

His voice was raw and scratchy, both intimidating and sexy. It was clear why Katella fell for the guy, on top of the fact that he sponsored the local animal shelters and women's shelters. The genuine tone made Harper smile to herself and it felt good to be protected by someone she didn't really know. But because she was part of this team, even from an administrative side, they looked at her as though she were one of their own and she really appreciated that sense of belongingness that gave her.

"He's right," Zach said, keeping his eyes in front of him. They were hard, guarded, looking every which way to keep a look out for Bryan. "Plus, I get a bad feeling from the guy other than the fact that he's a dick. I'll take you home, Xander will take Kat home and he'll meet me at my place and take me to my car. Then, I'll drive by your place to make sure you're okay."

"I can take" -

"God, I hate when women claim they can take care of themselves," he said. They start heading to the parking structure and Harper didn't feel afraid. Somehow, even with Bryan directly interacting with her, she didn't feel afraid. Somehow, Zach made her feel capable. Secure. She liked being around him, she realized. Even when he was being a jerk. "I'm not saying you can't take care of yourself. I don't know you well but you come across as a woman who is fully capable of making competent decisions and I'm assuming you possess the rare personality trait of common sense. But that doesn't mean I don't want to help you take care of yourself."

The line was still long even after one in the morning but the parking structure was somewhat empty. Katella and Xander said goodbye and it wasn't long before Harper was left with Zach alone.

"Can I ask you a question?" he asked as she led him to her car. It wasn't too far away, which was nice because they didn't have to walk far. She didn't have time to respond before he said, "Why did you go out with that guy?"

Harper felt a prickle of discomfort at the direct question. To be honest, she didn't think it was any of his business why she chose to be with someone, especially considering Zach hadn't even known her before then. It wasn't as though she started asking about the rumors that followed him from the Toronto Bangles to here.

"Look," Zach said through a sigh. Harper could feel his crystal blue eyes on her profile but she refused to look at him, not until she had something she could say to him. "I'm not trying to judge you. Hell, my choice in girlfriends - if you could even call them that - is questionable, to say the least. You just, you just don't seem like the type of girl who would even tolerate that jackass's bullshit."

Now she did have a reason to speak to him. "And what type of girl do you think I am?" she asked, glancing at him quickly before fixing her eyes back to the road.

Zach shrugged. "To tell you the truth, I don't know," he said. "I've been drinking, I tend to ramble even more than I already do, I barely know you. All I know is your attractive, you're smart, and despite your best efforts, you're a good dancer. I've never seen anyone wear plaid to a nightclub before but somehow you manage to pull it off, you're an excellent writer and you don't need the typical bullshit drama to get people to read your stuff, and you have eyes I've never seen before. Also, you challenge me in a way I've never been challenged before so, I figure, if you won't put up with my bullshit, you definitely shouldn't be putting up with his, especially since I'm so much better looking."

Harper snorted despite herself.

"See? I made you laugh," he said. "Now you have to tell me."

"Oh, I do?" Harper said, shifting her eyes over at him once she was forced to slow down due to a red light. His eyes were closed and his body was slouched against the leather seat of her car. He was ready to pass out any second. Good thing he was taking a cab home. That, and he wasn't driving now.

Somehow, through the haze, he nodded. His eyes remained shut. "Please," he added. Now Harper knew he was drunk - he would never say please otherwise. "I want to know how someone like you could be with someone like that. Your dad not around?"

Any fleeting moments of happiness were dashed in that off-handed compliment. "Actually," she said, her voice cold - colder than she intended but she wasn't sorry about it. She felt her walls spring back up, defending her against his question even though, moments before, she actually felt prepared to answer him. "My dad's dead. My mom, too." She looked straight ahead, her eyes lifeless. She could see her leasing office from where she was under the streetlights. She would be home soon, in bed.

She could hear Zach swallow, and then, "Harp, I'm so" –

"It's fine," she said. She pulled up to her building, into her parking spot.

"I didn't know," he said. To his credit, he did sound genuine.

"No one does, really," she said. She turned to him, and the look on his face – pleading and regretful – almost made her crack. Almost. "Thanks for" –

"Stop," he said. "Don't do that."

She raised a brow. "Do what?" she asked.

He gave her a face. "Shut me out," he told her. "I may not have gone to college but I'm not an idiot. I know what you're doing."

"And what am I doing?"

"Shutting me out."

"My parents died."

Zach blinked, swallowed. His skin went pale and he looked sober in that moment. "I'm sorry," he said, his voice raw and regretful. He actually sounded like he meant it. "Can I ask" -

"DUI."

Every time Harper said it, it got easier to say the next time. Regardless, she didn't like talking about it, especially to people she didn't know very well. She didn't like people to look at her a certain way or make judgments about her life because of one major piece of her puzzle. She absolutely hated the whispers, the sympathetic faces, the stale apologies when people found out. As such, she didn't like telling anyone. Bryan didn't find out until six months into their relationship and it was because her grandmother brought it up, not because Harper chose to share it directly.

For some reason, she decided to continue a bit. Maybe because Zach seemed genuinely interested in what she had to say. Maybe it was to avoid any further questions he would have, and while she didn't know Zach well, she did know he had a penchant for asking questions.

"They had this weekly date night," she said, her eyes shooting out of the windshield rather than stare at Zach. "They were crazy for one another. Couldn't keep their hands off of each other, teased each other mercilessly but always had each other's back. Gross for me as a kid but it's relationship goals for me. I stayed with my dad's mom, my grandma, whenever they went on a date. One day, when I was fourteen, they never came back. So I stayed with my grandmother always. I never drink. I don't go out too often at night at places that have a big night scene because I don't want to put myself in a situation where something could happen."

He nodded a couple of times but made no move to say something or even leave.

"My mom cheated on my dad," he finally said, rolling his head so he could look at her. "He found out and didn't leave her but she kept doing it behind his back to the point where she didn't even hide it at all. I wanted to be out of my house at all costs because I hated my mom but weirdly enough, I hated my dad even more because it was like he was letting it happen. I lost respect for him. I don't really talk to them if I can help it except when my dad asks for tickets to the games. They're back in Canada now. It's one of the reasons I wanted a trade."

"Oh."

"Let me guess," he said, a lofty smile on his face that didn't quite reach his eyes. "You think it's because I slept with Toner's wife."

"I didn't say that," Harper said.

"You didn't have to." Was it her imagination or did he actually seem disappointed in her?

"I don't care why you're here," she said. "The point is, you are. To answer your question, Bryan was never like the way he is now when we first started dating."

"They never are," he said with a soft smile, his eyes going over her seatbelt strapped against her chest.

"So if you know that, why even ask?"

He shrugged his broad shoulders. "Just making conversation, I guess," he said with a sardonic grin. "I just get defensive when I see someone talk to their significant other that way. I wasn't lying when I told him I would rip him to shreds. You know that, right?"

"Why do you care?" Harper asked, pressing her brows together. "You barely know me. Why are you putting all of this effort into someone you barely even know?"

He stared at Harper for a long moment, his crystal blue eyes taking in every detail her face had to offer – her big eyes, her high cheeks, her full lips, the freckles on the bridge of her nose, the scar just above her eyebrow she got after falling from a bike. She felt her cheeks warm up under his scrutiny and she was sure her face was pink – as it usually got when people stared. She didn't like the feeling for the most part, but with Zach, it was studious rather than sleazy.

"I like you," he said finally. He reached out and started fiddling with the hemline of Harper's shirt. "You're different. I guess I want to learn more about you."

Harper swallowed. She wasn't sure how to react to an honest statement. In fact, she wasn't prepared for it.

"Well," she said, because she had to say something, especially with the way he was looking at her. The atmosphere had gotten heavy, suffocating, but not in a bad way. In a way where Zach's lips would be her only option in acquiring oxygen. "Thank you. For what you did. You didn't have to, you know."

Without warning, Zach leaned toward her and placed a quick kiss on her cheek. "I can walk you up, you know," he said. "My cab will be here in a couple" –

At that moment, two headlights sliced through their solitary darkness.

"Right now," he amended.

Harper got out of her car, followed by Zach.

"Thank you," she said again, and she genuinely meant it.

"Anytime." He sounded like he meant it as well.

Harper headed up to her unit, but before she opened the door, she looked over her shoulder, only to find Zach standing by the cab, the back door open and waiting for him, watching her go inside. She raised an arm, waved, and finally turned in for the night.

Chapter 10

WHEN HARPER WOKE up the next morning, there was a voicemail on her phone. Either she hadn't heard her phone go off or she forgot to turn on the ringer. Either way, she stretched and stood up, grabbing her phone and playing the message.

"What's up, Crawford? Just want to make sure you're okay. I didn't see any assholes lingering outside your place or anything. Call me when you wake up. Have a good night. And by the way, you're a decent dancer. In fact, I would dance with you again. You know. If I had to."

Harper felt her lips curl up into a smile despite herself. Was she actually starting to like him? The warm, gooey feeling dripped inside of her like caramel and she couldn't push it away. She hesitated in calling him, however. She didn't know why, but the thought of calling him to talk to him not in a professional capacity made butterflies start to flutter out of their cacoons and fly around her stomach. Which was dumb since it reminded her of having a crush on someone in high school. She felt juvenile and foolish and this was the last thing she should feel.

"He's just concerned," she muttered to herself as she padded into the kitchen in order to grab herself some coffee. She needed coffee if she was going to wake up fully. "You can call him. He said to. And now I'm talking to myself like a totally sane person... Not."

She started making her coffee before grabbing her phone and immediately dialing Zach's number just to get it over with. There was a chance that he might be asleep. There was a chance he wouldn't answer. There was a chance he won't even recognize her number. There were lots of chances for a lot of different things. There was one possibility that he would actually answer.

And he did.

"Hello?"

"Hey." A beat, and then Harper rolled her eyes at herself. "It's Harper."

"Yeah, I know." She could hear a smirk in his voice and she rolled her eyes again.

"I'm calling you back."

"Okay."

Silence. Awkward silence hung between them and drove Harper completely up the wall. She glared at her coffee machine like it was someone else's fault and decided she should have had coffee in her before calling him back.

"Okay," she said, running her fingers through her hair. "Well, I'm fine so thanks again for yesterday. Have a good" -

"Do you want to grab breakfast?"

Well. That was surprising.

"What?"

"Well, I'm hungry," he explained. "I'm sure you're hungry. I owe you for last night. I'm new here. You're not. You can show me around."

"Oh." She cleared her throat. Her coffee was ready. She didn't trust herself to pour a cup, afraid her fingers would shake and she would spill the hot liquid everywhere. She was already bad, drinking it in a stationary position. Now, holding a phone, being asked on a date – was it a date? – she wouldn't know what to do with herself.

"You don't owe me for last night," she found herself saying before she could stop and think about it. "There's nothing to owe"

"Yeah," he corrected, his voice insistent. "There is. I don't like to admit it but I was a jackass. I talk a lot. Even more when I drink. I said some dumb things because I'm trying to understand how a girl like you could end up with a guy like that douche."

"I wasn't a victim of circumstance, Zach," she told him, though she wasn't defending Bryan or even herself. "I know you might think you're complimenting me by contrasting someone like me with Bryan, but honestly, it comes out snarky and judgmental. I dated him when I was young and in college, and even though we broke up only eight months ago, I'm a very different person than I was back then. I chose to be with Bryan. Each time I think about that choice – because I distinctly remember it like it was yesterday – my insides curl up and I literally want to wretch the contents of my stomach everywhere. People say don't have regrets because things get you where you are. I say that's all bullshit. Bryan was the biggest mistake of my life but it was a mistake I made and a mistake I stuck with." Harper paused in order to catch her breath. Her eyes were shining with tears she refused to shed. When she regained more control of her voice, she took another breath. In a low voice, she said, "Bryan was different *before* we got serious, like all guys are. It wasn't until we were serious that I realized how he truly was. By then, I was in too deep and my pride wouldn't let me give up all the time I wasted with him. So I wasted even more time. Until I decided I was done."

"What made you decide?" His voice was quiet and gentle, not pushy.

Harper swallowed. She had never told anybody this, not even her closest friends. "Honestly?" she asked.

"Honestly," he said. "I want to know."

"I hated myself when I looked into the mirror," she said. The tears did fall now, rolling off her cheeks in slow tracks until they gathered at the tip of her chin. "I didn't want to be her anymore. And the one thing I knew I needed to change was the person who made me feel awful about myself. And that was him."

There was a heavy silence, and Harper shook her head at herself, ramming her palm into her forehead. She shouldn't have told him. She should have accepted his date and kept her mouth shut. Dating 101: never talk about your ex, even if your date wanted to know.

Then, "So. Breakfast?"

They got off the phone with a plan to meet at a small mom and pop diner that had cheap food, was right on the beach, and would be quiet this early in the morning – especially on a Friday. Harper spent more time than usual deciding on what to wear – she decided on skinny jeans and an over-sized white sweatshirt that dipped low in front. She tossed her hair up into a messy ponytail, and put on light makeup that might or might not emphasize her eyes. She grabbed her keys and drove past Fifteenth Street, parking in front of a small, beachside Catholic church. She got there first and decided to get out of the car and take a seat at the picnic benches in the sand, just in front of the diner. She grabbed one with an umbrella, just in case the sun decided to peak through the overcast sky.

The diner wasn't as busy at it usually got on the weekends, especially during the summer. Since tourist season was simmering away into fall, there was a slight decline in beach visitors, which was what Harper preferred.

While she waited for Zach, her mind drifted back to last night – technically, this morning. She couldn't help but replay the scene over and over again: Zach holding onto her, pulling her close so her back hit his chest; grabbing his neck with her arm and running her fingers through his hair; tilting her head away, causing Zach's lips to brush her neck.

They had been dancing – Harper *never* danced!

She shook her head, crossing her arms over her chest and shifting her weight consistently in order to keep warm. Not only had they danced, but she told him everything. About her parents, at least. She told him about Bryan. She told him… a lot. More than she liked to tell. She didn't understand how that happened. Maybe she was just tired and that gave way to poor, thoughtless choices. Maybe he had some kind of superpower. Maybe she trusted him already, which would be ridiculous and naïve.

"Hey."

Harper spun around, only to see Zach standing there in board shorts, flip-flops, and a black v-neck.

"Aren't you cold?" she asked, giving him a look as she stood up. She wasn't sure if she should hug him or not.

"I'm from Toronto," he said, his voice flat. Zach had no question about whether or not he should hug her – he pulled her into his arms without hesitation. Her face was buried in his chest and he smelled of rich cologne, masculine and fresh. Clean. She liked it. "This is not cold."

He let his arms linger longer than necessary and she didn't break away from him. He leaned down and kissed the top of her head.

"So," he said, and they seemed to break apart simultaneously, "let's grab some food. I'm starving."

Harper's stomach rumbled in response and she led him into the small restaurant. She didn't worry about someone grabbing their bench – there were plenty of picnic tables with or without umbrellas that were still unoccupied.

The two ordered their food quickly – she ordered a Belguim waffle with fresh fruit and no whip cream and a cup of water, he ordered a Spanish omelet that came with a side of breakfast potatoes with a coffee – and Zach made sure to pay before

Harper could even offer to split the check. Once his coffee was made with three creams and three sugars, they headed back out and took a seat on the same bench that overlooked the horizon. There was a crisp Newport Beach breeze that was typical for the beach suburb, and even though it was busy, it wasn't overwhelming. There was enough space to breathe and relax.

"How did you know about this place?" he asked, twisting his torso so he faced her.

"My mom used to take me a while back when I was a kid every Sunday morning," she explained, curling locks of hair behind her ear. "She used to call it our Mother-Daughter date. After she died, my grandmother would take me, but it wasn't the same, you know?"

He nodded, his hands in the pockets of his board shorts. "You took me here," he pointed out.

She nodded, looking at him from the corner of her eye. "Yes," she agreed.

"Why?" he asked. "It was a special place for you and your mom. Why invite me to it?"

"Special places shouldn't be kept hidden," she said. "They should be shared. Just because I was emotional with my grandma doesn't mean I will be with you. It's been years since my parents died."

"Yeah, but it doesn't get any easier."

"No, you're right about that."

"Zach!" the waitress called, holding a plastic tray filled with paper plates of steaming hot food. Zach waved his arm and she walked over to them in the sand before passing out their food.

When she was gone, Zach proceeded to dig in. Harper had to press her lips together to keep from laughing out loud at the spectacle he was making of himself. It was as though he hadn't had any food in the past forty-eight hours. She knew hockey players needed the calories but it hadn't hit her until that moment, staring at Zach. She shook her head, allowing herself to smile, before grabbing the syrup and dousing it on her waffle.

Breakfast was silent, for the most part. Harper and Zach were too busy eating to really make conversation, and that was okay with them. It wasn't awkward or tense; it was relaxing and comfortable. Harper could see herself doing this again should the occasion call for it.

After they finished, Zach suggested they go for a walk. "I'm renting one of these homes," he told her. "I'd love to see my neighborhood."

Harper wasn't sure if he was just saying that as an excuse to prolong their date – which he absolutely did not have to do – or if he was being genuine. Either way, she allowed him to take hold of her hand after they threw away their trash and walk with her up and down the Balboa boardwalk. He didn't let go, and neither did she.

Chapter 11

HARPER DIDN'T WANT to admit it, but the minute she got home from her impromptu date with Zach, she did a happy dance after ensuring the door was closed and locked. He had come from nowhere, and perhaps a part of her would still be in denial about this growing *thing* that was happening between them. She didn't want to say it was feelings because she wasn't quite sure how she felt about the star center, but she also could not deny that she was attracted to him. He was tall, muscled, and primal – there were times she noticed him staring at her like she was already his, even though they had barely been on a date. Which should have scared her, that he was already territorial over her and they weren't even dating. But maybe he was just protective over all the women in his life. Maybe he was like this with all the women he dated.

The thought was like an icy bucket of water was thrown onto her. He had dated many women. Rumors followed him even here, about messing with the wife of a former teammate. Regardless of the validity of those rumors, there had to be a kernel of truth buried somewhere in there.

Maybe Harper should still be on her guard. She didn't know

what he was thinking, what he felt, and it wouldn't be wise to allow herself to get swept off of her feet so soon. Not until she had her head on straight. Not until she knew his intentions.

And who knew? Perhaps he wasn't exactly the sort of guy she would even want to be with. First and foremost, he was a professional athlete, which was akin to being a high-paid jock in high school. The type of women they were supposed to end up with was not who Harper was and she wouldn't sacrifice her identity to be with a guy who might very well cheat on her.

Okay, maybe that wasn't fair. Not all professional athletes were cheaters. And just because Bryan turned out to be a dick didn't mean Zach was. Even if rumors said otherwise. Maybe she was just trying to protect herself. Maybe she wanted to ensure she didn't get hurt again, and as much as she wanted to try this out with Zach, she knew it would end in heartbreak. And Zach was someone she worked with, someone she would see at work every day unless she quit, got fired, or he was traded.

This wasn't a good idea. No matter how good it felt.

She shook her head. She needed a shower and to change. She had a meeting with Seraphina, and considering they just had their first exhibition game and Harper had written about it meant she was going to get her first official feedback from her boss. Maybe she could focus her nervous energy into that rather than in Zach. Lord knew he already had a big head. She didn't need to make it bigger, whether he knew it or not.

⸺

SERAPHINA LOOKED as though she had been in her office since the early morning, but somehow, she still appeared fresh-faced and beautiful. Her cheeks were rosy, her eyes were bright – only made up by the black mascara lengthening her lashes – and her lips were glossed pink. She wore a navy blue dress that tied at the waist and reached her knee in soft, plated strips. On her feet was a pair of nude heels. Harper wished she was as fashionable as Seraphina was, but her dark jeans and white collared shirt were nothing in comparison.

"Harper," Seraphina said with a warm smile and a sparkle in her eyes. "It's so good to see you. Come in, come in." She used her fingers to beckon Harper in the office before gesturing at one of the chairs in front of her desk. "Thanks so much for coming in today. Your blazer is super cute."

"Oh." Harper glanced down at the black blazer, a light flush touching her cheeks. "Thank you."

"Of course," she said. "So, I wanted to talk to you about your travel assignments but first, I want to get your feedback. How are you?"

"I'm good," Harper asked.

Did Seraphina know about the date she and Zach went on earlier? No, there was no way. It just happened. Right? But Seraphina was powerful; it wouldn't surprise her to know that she somehow found out. Maybe Harper should tell her. Maybe she had done something wrong. She didn't want to compromise her job or her friendship with Seraphina. If she wasn't allowed to date Zach, she wouldn't.

"That's great, I'm glad to hear that." Seraphina was still smiling, a genuine gesture that made Harper feel guilty about something even though she didn't do anything wrong. "How's the writing coming along? Can I be honest with you – I have no idea how you do it. Coming up with new, fresh ideas every week. I am so lucky to have you as our blogger and social media expert."

"It's nothing big," Harper said.

"Don't be humble," Seraphina said. "Own what you do. You are great at a job that could easily have fallen flat. You aren't easily replaceable, Harper. Don't take that for granted." She leaned back in her chair. "I'm not trying to lecture you, Harper. I'm just trying to make you realize how amazing you are. I feel like people in this profession treat it just like it's a business. I get it. It works. It is a business. My grandfather did the same thing. But once I inherited the team, after my grandfather…" She swallowed, her eyes on the surface of her desk rather than on Harper. Harper couldn't blame her. "I wanted to be taken seriously in this business. So I went back to school and got my Masters. My favorite class was Outside Business Practices, which talked about different business tracks to get the most out of your consumer and out of your employees. Positive reinforcement, genuine tokens of appreciation, were rarely used in the business industry even though it's common sense: you encourage your employees, they're going to *want* to work for you, right? So that's what I'm trying to do with you, Harper. With everyone I see. You are a stellar writer. You could be a sports journalist if you wanted. I just wanted to take the time to remind you how important you are to us."

Harper wasn't quite sure how to respond. She felt her face take flame and couldn't help but drop her eyes to her lap. With that, however, came pride. Pride in her work and her passion, but also pride in working for someone like Seraphina Hanson.

"How are you?" Harper asked, quirking a brow and finally picking her eyes up to meet Seraphina's. "I know you're good about checking in on us but who checks in on you?"

Seraphina shot Harper a knowing smile. "Touché," she agreed. "I will admit, it has been difficult maintaining friendships through this transitional phase for me. I'm handling it as best as I can."

Harper gave Seraphina a look. "Seraphina, I know you're my boss and I appreciate the dedication to professionalism you maintain," she said, "but I want you to feel you can confide in me if you need to. Maybe it's still too early to call each other friends but I'd like to try. I mean, I did pick up your sister from a club the other night."

Seraphina shook her head. "Can you believe Kat?" she asked, her eyes going wide. "Oh my God, when I heard she was actually partying with everyone…" She let her voice trail off and crossed her arms over her chest. "I mean, I can't imagine what she's going through. Star center breaks up with her and we trade him and there's a chance we might get him again. I also know she's trying to be strong for my sake, to take one for the team, literally. But I just wish she'd be more honest with her feelings. Like when Peters and she were over, she couldn't just tell me she missed him. I knew she did, obviously, but she would never admit it. Her pride is going to be her downfall, let me tell you." She pushed her brow up. "I am so sorry, I'm babbling."

Harper laughed. "Don't worry about it," she said, waving Seraphina's apology away. "I do that when I'm nervous. Look, I can't imagine what you went through after your grandfather was murdered." Her eyes widened when she realized how callous that sounded. "I'm sorry, that was harsh. I'm a good writer but I can't seem to speak to save my life."

"No," Seraphina said, shaking her head. "I appreciate the directness. It's been a year and people still tiptoe around it like it didn't happen, which pisses me off because people don't think I can handle it, even now." She clenches her jaw. "The sexism" – she cut herself off and shook her head once more. "I can't even get into this right now. I'll work myself up." She forced a smile. "Thank you. For speaking to me like a human."

Harper smiled and nodded once. "Of course," she said. "If there's anything you need, anything I can do to help, please don't hesitate to let me know."

"I will," she said, her eyes flitting over to the windows in her office.

Seraphina's office was rare in that nearly every crevice of it was glass. Her grandfather created the designs himself, wanting to have a good view of the Pacific Ocean crashing into the shore. It was hard to be stressed in the office. The only touch of darkness was the stain of blood on the carpet underneath Harper's chair. Rumor had it that Katella wanted Seraphina to tear up the carpet and put in wood flooring to get rid of the blood, but Seraphina refused. She kept it there, as a reminder to her and to everyone else that her grandfather had died for this team and his death would not be in vain.

"So," Seraphina said, snapping her eyes back to Harper. "Let's talk travel. As usual, the Gulls have a crappy travel schedule, even during the preseason. Anytime they travel, I want you to go with them, so you can write an article on something – whether it's a character article on the player, an article on the city, or a technical article on the game. It'll be tough when we have the back-to-back games – and it looks like we'll have quite a few of those – and I wanted to bring you in just to make sure it's something you feel you can handle. Not that I don't think you can, I just think it's important that I get your feedback as well."

Harper nodded. "I can handle it, for sure," she said. "It will be overwhelming but as long as I plan out potential articles in advanced, it shouldn't be a problem."

Seraphina smiled brightly. "Great," she said. "Well, that's what I wanted to call you in for. Unless there was something else you wanted to discuss."

Was it Harper's imagination, or did Seraphina seem like she knew where Harper had been this morning, and who Harper had been with? Her mouth dried up and she hoped she didn't look like a deer caught in headlights because that was exactly the way she felt.

Part of her wanted to talk to Seraphina about Zach, but it was too new and Harper didn't even know what she wanted. She didn't want to bring up an issue when there was no issue. Not yet, at least. And by talking about it, addressing it, gave it a seriousness she didn't think it possessed just yet. Who knew if she and Zach were going to go out again? Harper didn't want to start planning things for it to wind up biting her in the ass.

"No," she managed to say, hoping her voice didn't come out as shrill as it sounded and that she was being paranoid. "I think we're good."

Seraphina nodded. If she didn't believe Harper, it didn't

show. "Good," she said. "Thanks for coming in. I'll get you your flight information out to you tonight."

Harper smiled and left. She didn't want to think about the utter desire she had to share everything about Zach with Seraphina just so she could get excited about it with someone.

Chapter 12

ZACHARY RYAN LOVED EXHIBITION GAMES. He knew they didn't count and he knew a lot of his teammates used them as warm-up games, not playing their hardest, making sure to take it easy lest they get an injury before the actual season. Zach did not have that same mentality. Even though he would be the Gulls' first line center regardless of his performance during these games, the rookies and the draft picks would be fighting hard to get noticed. They pushed harder, shot with power, and played dirty.

He fed off of that. Especially these punk kids who thought they knew everything just because they won some trophy down with their U17 and U18 teams, just because they got drafted by a national hockey team, just because they were still and vital, just because girls started to throw themselves at them, just in case they turned out to be the next big thing in hockey. He liked knocking them down by a peg. He liked putting them in their place. And more than anything, he liked reminding them that with age came experience, wisdom, and strength.

He got to the Ice Palace an hour before call time. He liked to walk up and down each staircase in the terrace portion of the

75

rink. He would clear his mind and just count each and every step. His legs burned by the time he would finish, but he was warmed up and ready to skate. The exercise – superstition, if he was being honest calmed him so his muscles were relaxed and his mind was clear from everything – nerves, problems in his professional and personal lives, even Harper was temporarily removed from the forefront of his mind.

By the time his teammates trickled in, he was already lacing up his skates. They were the first pieces of equipment he put on, besides black tights, even though it would be difficult to pull on his shorts and the official Gulls' shells that went over the shorts. It was how he dressed himself for every practice, every game, every tournament. He didn't want anyone helping him, especially not his parents'.

Regardless, they would trickle into the locker room and impart sage advice to him before his game.

"Get the hard part over with," his mother would tell him, looking him in the eye. His own eyes, reflected back at him. "Then everything is easy-peasey."

He took his time getting dressed. There was a lot of equipment, a lot of Velcro and clear tape to hold up his socks. When he was a teenager, he was so skinny, he'd have to use some tape around his shorts, just to ensure they were tight at the waist. Shin guards, elbow pads, shoulder and chest pads over a t-shirt – a grey shirt with a green Superman logo – and then his official Gulls home jersey. It was a sleek navy blue with off-white lettering. On the front was a silver anchor, on the back was his last name above his number: **15**. Fifteen out of respect for Stevenson. Fifty-one since he was six and his mother scrawled a list of potential numbers and they randomly assigned him fifty-one. His helmet – no shield – was on his head but left unbuckled, and his black gloves were on even though they didn't need to be. Not yet.

Coach Cherney walked in at that moment, no-nonsense and business-oriented. He wasn't the typical sort of hockey coach –

he was small and slight, bald head and bushy mustache, but in the short amount of time Zach had known him, he knew Cherney didn't bullshit, was direct, and if a player needed it, had no problem calling him out for whatever he screwed up on. He didn't coddle but he didn't crack the whip unless it was deserved.

Cherney walked in the center of the locker room, careful not to step over or walk across the anchor logo stitched into the center of the floor. "All right, boys," he said in a deep voice, "it's our second exhibition game as a team. Some of you won't dress because you're assigned to various places across the Palace. Have fun interacting with the public." A couple of chuckles from the guys in suits rather than sweaters. "For those of you who are playing, stay focused but remember that you are more than the intensity of the game. I'm not going to tell you these games don't mean anything but if I see any one of you do something selfish, you'll be benched for however long I see fit. Got it?"

There were nods in assent, but nothing vocal. They were getting in the game, getting ready for that buzzer.

Cherney left to take his position on the bench, leaving the team alone in silence for the next few moments. Then, Thorpe stood, dressed in all the padding and equipment that made up being a goalie, and the guys followed him from the locker room down a short hallway and to the mouth of the rink.

Zach felt his heart start to pound like a drum in a rock song, steady and hard, over and over again. He could hear the booing of the crowd as the referees skated onto the ice, could hear the booing increase as the opposing team – the Los Angeles Stars – skated out there.

Then, the announcement. "Now, ladies and gentlemen, put your hands together for your Newport Beach Seagulls!"

Thorpe was out first, and the rest of the team followed. The minute Zach's skates touched the ice, he felt the adrenaline coursing through his bloodstream. He didn't look at the fans –

the building was considerably empty, considering it was only an exhibition game – and instead, looked ahead, at what was in front of him.

Zach also wouldn't look at the opposing team. It was one of the two rivalries the Gulls had so he knew that despite the fact that it didn't count, there was a measure of pride on the line, especially for the fans. It was his second game these people saw him play in a Gulls' sweater. He would make sure he took the rivalry seriously.

When the team finished their welcome skate around their half of the rink, the starting line up – three shooters, two defensemen, and one goalie – lined up on the blue line as the announcer raised the singing of the national anthem. Zach was used to two anthems being sung due to the fact that his former team had been Canadian, and anytime a Canadian team played an American team, both anthems were sung. Though he wasn't a citizen, he respected the anthem and what it represented. He had no problem standing and remaining silent during it. It reminded him to focus. Besides him, he noticed Kyle Underwood jump up and down, swinging his arm out while holding his stick with the other before switching.

Kyle Underwood, his line mate and one of the few remaining members of the Gulls pre-Seraphina. The guy was his age, maybe a few months younger than Zach. He was tall, blond, with clear blue eyes. He looked lean but Zach knew Underwood had solid muscle underneath the padding he wore. He had to, with the beating he took every game by standing in the goalie crease, trying to get his stick on a stray puck or a rebound. Plus, the guy was just a prick and opponents liked to take shots at him. Zach knew they would try to trip him up or crosscheck him.

Not that Underwood didn't deserve it. Kyle was known as an instigator. Everyone hated him unless he was on their team. He was skilled and had no problem answering if he was ever called to fight. He rarely if ever smiled on the ice, instead choosing to focus on the game. Zach respected him and was glad he could call him teammate now.

When the anthem was over, Zach jumped once, twice, shaking out any loose nerves and started skating around his side of the ice, just to loosen his muscles. When the refs blew their whistles, he leaned forward, his hands holding his stick horizontally as he skated to center ice. He refused to look at Drew Browning, didn't want the guy to have any chance of getting in his head.

Zach stood straight and got his stick ready. The whistle blew. The puck dropped. Zach reached with his stick and won the faceoff to start the game.

Harper couldn't take her eyes off of Zach while he played. She had seen him before, of course, when he used to play for Toronto, but there was something magical about watching him play for her team. He wasn't the fastest skater but that was partly because his body was muscled and strong. He made up for it in brute force. He, like his linemate Kyle Underwood wasn't afraid to do to the corners of the rink and mix it up in order to retrieve the puck. He had no problem body checking, shoving, and throwing his hips out in order to make a play.

He was mesmerizing.

Zach Ryan had his flaws. Like, she noted, he wasn't fast but he was strong. He didn't shoot the puck when he had opportunities, instead choosing to pass it. His passes, however, were crisp and perfect, almost always ending up to his teammate exactly where the teammate needed it to be in order to get a shot on goal. Every now and then, he would drop a pass back without looking to see if it hit its target, and most of the time, the opposing team would swoop in and intercept it. Zach got too cute, too cocky, in his passing.

During the commercial breaks, Harper narrowed her eyes

from her seat at center ice to try and gauge what sort of player he was when the cameras weren't rolling and the game wasn't in play. If he was on the ice and the Ice Princesses were sweeping up the ice in order to smooth it out, she didn't notice him checking them out – even though she couldn't blame him if he did. They were all gorgeous, in uniforms that left little to the imagination.

He did tend to spit a lot, however. And every now and then, he would clear out his nose while on the bench, while the cameras were on him. It was disgusting, but he didn't even seem to care. Which, oddly enough, was kind of attractive. The blatant disregard for what people thought of him was a turn on. It was almost as though when he played, his attention and focus remained there. He did what he had to do in order to play his best, be it spitting, clearing his nose, or ignoring the entire rink and focus on that little rubber puck.

"What do you think?" her grandmother asked from her side in a low murmur, once the buzzer sounded and the skaters headed back to the locker room.

Zach was so close to her, if he just looked up, he would see her. Except he didn't. And Harper's respect for him grew.

Right now, the game was the only thing that mattered. Right now, that was the only thing that should matter. She didn't want to be the girl that distracted the athlete during a game, even an exhibition one. Her pride didn't take a hit because of it. In fact, she preferred it that way. It showed her he had his priorities in order.

"I think he's amazing," she responded honestly. And Harper meant every word.

Chapter 13

THE MINUTE their home game ended and their fans cleared out, the team was forced to shower, change, and were ushered onto a bus and driven to the John Wayne Airport. They flew to Arizona on the team's private jet, and everyone took the hour flight to try and catch some sleep. Zach noticed Harper in the back, reading on her kindle, but since she didn't acknowledge him, he didn't acknowledge her. Didn't want to disturb her if she was in the middle of something important.

Zach hadn't put too much thought in their date. He refused to overthink things. All he knew was that he liked being around Harper. There was something different about her, something he could relate to, something that kept him grounded despite the fact that there was nothing really tying them together, save for one date. The problem was, as much as he tried not to think about her, when she was around him, he couldn't stop staring. Golden brown hair, forest green eyes, freckles. The quintessential girl next door and exactly his type. Petite. Curvy. Long legs. The only flaw she seemed to possess was her unruly hair – it was wavy, which made it look messy when it wasn't. But that wasn't a deal breaker and it wasn't something he particularly cared about. In fact, it reminded him of sex hair, and he was all about sex hair.

"Hey, man." He picked his eyes up and Oscar Solis, one of his teammates – an offensive defenseman paired with Zach's line on the ice – stood next to his seat. "The team's going to go to this local club – the Phoenix Club – and wanted to know if you wanted to join us."

Typically, Zach would have said no. They had a game tomorrow night and he wanted to get sleep. But it was an excuse to get closer to Harper, to touch her, to dance with her again. He didn't like to use the fact that it was an exhibition game because even though they didn't technically count, Zach still took them seriously. Any time he had the opportunity to get on the ice, he took it and skated his hardest, whether he won or played well or not. Maybe it was because he used hockey as a way to escape his family drama, and when he was invited to try out for a travel team, it actually got him far away from them.

He wouldn't waste ice time, not even as an NHL player. Not even an exhibition game.

It would force him to work harder tomorrow, but if he made it worthwhile tonight, it would be worth it.

His eyes flickered over to Harper, still reading, before going back to Solis. "I'm in," he said with a grin.

———

CONVINCING HARPER TOOK MUCH MORE time than Zach thought it would initially. After they checked into their hotel rooms and he dropped off his stuff, he immediately went to Harper's room. She was lucky she didn't have to room with anyone, but his roommate, Solis, assured him he wouldn't be back until the early morning. To be honest, Zach didn't know if it was because he was a few years shy of thirty, but he couldn't party all night the way he used to. And he didn't intend to. All he cared about was getting Harper into his arms, pressed against his body, for the rest of the night. Maybe he'd have a couple of drinks, but she was his only goal.

At first, she had refused, citing she was a morning person and needed sleep. Then, she told him she wasn't a party girl. Finally, Zach promised an exclusive interview regarding the rumors that followed him from Toronto. She gave in and got dressed in an hour.

When Zach came to her door, he could not take his eyes off of her. Which was saying something, considering he typically couldn't take his eyes off of her. She straightened her hair, did her makeup, and the slip of a dress wasn't even worthy of being called a dress – the straps were thin, the front was low and the hemline was short – so short it just barely covered her behind, revealing long legs in simple black stilettos.

Fuck, she looked amazing.

"Ready?" she asked with a small smile, as though she knew the affect she had on him.

He almost grinned in response. Two could play at that.

Zach had a cab waiting as they walked out of the hotel. He opened the door for her and slid in afterward.

"Phoenix Club," Zach murmured to the driver.

The drive was ten minutes with no traffic, and even though it was just after ten o'clock, there was already a long line around the building. Zach almost hesitated. He didn't know if people actually knew who he was, and he knew Harper already thought he was an arrogant prick so dropping his name at the door wouldn't help that part of his reputation. However, it would be a waste of a night if they had to wait in line, and due to the goosebumps littering her skin, he could tell she was already cold.

"Zach," a voice called from the crowd. "Zach!"

Zach took a step toward the voice and saw Solis and a few other players at the front of the line. They were all dressed in dark jeans and collared shirts, similar to his own attire, waving him over. He grinned, releasing a breath he didn't realize he had been holding as subtly as possible.

He could feel Harper hesitate as he placed a hand on the small of her back, guiding her towards his teammates.

"We're going in a group?" she asked, her voice catching.

"Yeah," he told her. "Is that a problem?"

"No."

She shook her head, avoiding his eyes. She was lying to him, he knew, but he would get to the bottom of it eventually. Maybe she wanted him all to herself. Maybe she wanted something more low key, more romantic. He pressed his lips together and looked straight ahead. He just assumed going out in a group would be easier than going out just the two of them, especially since they had already gone on a date.

Zach decided not to think about it any longer. Instead, he reached his hand toward hers and entwined his fingers with hers. She squeezed back, giving him a smile. Any hesitation, any doubt, had left her delicate features. He couldn't tell if that was because she didn't care anymore or if it was because she was good at hiding how she was feeling.

He hoped not. He hoped she would feel comfortable enough to tell him what she was truly feeling.

They didn't speak the entire way to the dance floor. The bodyguards patted him down and went through Harper's purse but didn't charge at all. The couple walked in with Zach's teammate to low lighting, pounding music, and a bigger dancefloor than Taboo's. His teammates, Solis and Berringer, were already looking at the beautiful women who kept a sharp eye on them the minute they walked in. Zach couldn't tell if they were genuinely attracted to them or if they knew the guys were hockey players. Either way, Solis and Berringer sure as hell weren't complaining. If Zach had been by himself, he wouldn't have minded it, either. It felt good to be noticed, good to be desired. The motive behind that desire was simply semantics.

The problem was, Harper completely changed that. Now, he

only cared about impressing her, about being desired by her. He couldn't care less what anyone else thought of him as long as she liked him.

Which was so utterly middle school, he was almost sick with himself.

He refused to think about that. Not right now. Not when he just wanted to be near her.

Zach didn't even talk to the guys he was supposed to have come here with in the first place. Somehow, she read his mind. Somehow, she knew where he wanted to go. She let him lead her to the floor. He didn't need to buy her a drink first. There was no reason for small talk or empty flattery – though Zach would never have to lie when flattering her like he had to for some of the other women he had been with.

Harper was the most gorgeous woman he had ever seen. Aesthetically, perhaps he knew women who were more flawless. But for some reason, he couldn't keep his eyes off of her. He couldn't keep himself from not touching her when he was around. There was something about her that drew him to her like a moth to a flame.

He was in trouble and he knew it. And he didn't care.

The minute they were on the dance floor, the music surrounded them, fused through the bloodstream, and vibrated throughout their body. His hands found her waist and pulled her to him, so their pelvises were touching like magnets. It wasn't skin but it would have to do. For now.

He couldn't even say what song was playing. It didn't matter. All he cared about was getting Harper in his arms, pressing his body against hers, feeling her move against him. She knew how to move, despite her shyness, despite her hesitation. It was almost like a secret weapon. Looking at her forest green eyes, her chestnut brown hair, the freckles on her face, she looked like the quintessential good girl. An innocent. But the way she moved… There was more to her than the way she looked.

Without warning, she flipped around in his arms so her back

was pressed against his chest and her hips were rocking against his crotch. He had to think of something terrible in order to calm himself down or else he was going to lose it and press his hardness against her. The last thing he wanted her to think about was the fact that he might lose control around her. He wasn't a kid anymore, even though that was exactly how she made him feel.

Harper's arms reached up locked around his neck, bringing his head down over her left shoulder. Her back was arched up so he got a delicious view of her cleavage from where he stood, and didn't hesitate to take advantage of it.

God, her body.

Her hips rocked in time with the beat. How was she able to focus on the beat when there was this attraction, this pull, between the two of them. It was like a spell she cast around him, pulling him under her magic, making her irresistible. He couldn't resist her. He didn't even want to. All that was left to do was claim her as his.

So he did.

His lips found her shoulder and he could feel (thanks to his palms pressed flat on her stomach) her suck in a breath. He waited but did not stop his ministrations on her neck, wanting to see just how she would respond. There was a good chance she would push him off of her, and he would take the knock to his arrogance in stride, the way he always did when things didn't pan out the way he wanted them to.

But she didn't pull away. In fact, now that he noticed it, Harper's back was arched up, her head tilting away in order to give him more access to that beautiful column of her throat.

She wanted this. She wanted him just as badly.

He groaned as he felt himself stiffen upon this realization.

Without thinking, without waiting, he removed his lips from her skin and spun her around until they were face to face. He couldn't wait, didn't want to see the doubt and the rejection in her eyes. He would take what he wanted and deal with the consequences later. He might not have another chance.

After a beat, he grabbed her behind the head and pulled her to him, so he could kiss her mouth with as much fire as she caused in his very bones.

Chapter 14

HARPER'S EYES widened the minute his lips crashed onto hers. He was kissing her. It wasn't gentle. It was anything but. It reminded her of the way the ocean's waves crashed into the shore during a storm. And the best thing she could do was relax into the strong current and let the ocean pull her away. So her eyes closed and her arms wrapped around his neck and she opened her mouth, granting him a rare treat of being able to take in her taste, to duel for dominance, to really feel her.

His tongue was strong and determined, and when she put up a fight, he had no problem meeting her challenge. His hand was holding her head in place, his fingers clinging to the tresses tightly, a painful pull on her head causing her to hiss. Harper felt him grin in triumph through their kiss. The bastard actually grinned.

Two could play at this game.

Harper dropped her hands from his neck and put them on his chest, pushing him backward until he hit the wall behind him. The hallway was secluded; no one was around so she didn't have to worry about prying eyes or camera phones – if anyone even recognized Zachary Ryan. They certainly wouldn't recognize her. Then, once he had something solid behind him, she stepped between his legs and pushed her body against him. He groaned in surprise, a noise she found she liked. A noise she wanted to hear again.

His other hand dropped to her back, clawing at it to push her even closer to his body. Harper didn't even know how that was possible. There was no space between them where even the air couldn't breathe.

When they finally had to breathe, they grasped the oxygen like desperate divers with no air left in their tanks. Zach wasted no time in finding the skin on her neck with his mouth, sucking and gnawing and kissing and licking and whatever else he could do to evoke her ragged breathing and her gasping moans. She clung to his shirt with white knuckles and even though she was positive he was going to leave marks on her flesh like they were middle schoolers, she couldn't bring herself to care all that much. At least, not right now. She angled her neck away, giving him more access to her skin, and he took her up on the offer without any hesitation.

His hand slid to her shoulder, his fingers splayed as he gripped her collarbone, her heart hammering against his hand. She wondered if he could feel it beat, wondered if he realized he was causing her to react in this way. It was his fault. He had to have known it.

His hand dropped further and it cupped her breast, not too rough to hurt but just enough to let her know that he thought this, her body, was his to do whatever he liked with it. She arched into his touch and he squeezed, causing her to gasp. The dress she was wearing barely covered her breasts so she felt the warmth of his hand, the calluses on his palm, the possessive grip.

She gripped his shirt and pulled him to her, capturing his mouth with hers, letting him know that she approved of his touch, that she wanted more. He grunted through the kiss, and she knew she was reacting the way he wanted. She could feel him pressing insistently against her thigh, all but yelling at the reaction she caused inside of him. Her heart tripped over the pride that coursed through her body at being the reason for this, at rendering Zachary Ryan helpless.

Harper wanted to do more, cause him to make more of those sounds. She kept her mouth on his but dropped her right hand from his shirt and trailed it downward until her palm pressed against his member through the denim material of his jeans.

Zach tore his lips away, his hooded eyes heavy and dangerous. He couldn't even hold his head upright – he rested his forehead against hers. "Don't start something," he said through heavy breathing, "that you can't finish."

Her eyes were sharp, offended that he would make such an insinuation. She wrapped her fingers around him and squeezed. "I never do," she assured him.

He groaned helplessly, his eyes rolling to the back of his head. "Let's go," he managed to get out, "before I fuck you against this wall without giving a shit about who sees."

They managed to keep their hands to themselves in the cab, through the lobby, even in the elevator. For whatever reason, they wound up back at Zach's room, even though he had a roommate and she did not. But Solis wouldn't bring back a girl and Zach made sure to hang the Do Not Disturb sign on the door so even if Solis did come back earlier than expected, he would know the room was occupied.

When they were in the room, Harper looked at him with wide eyes. He didn't know her well enough to know if she was suddenly hesitating now that they were alone, in a bedroom, or if she was adjusting to the darkness.

"Do you want the lights on?" he asked.

"It doesn't matter," she replied.

For whatever reason, that made his temper react. It should matter. This would be their first time, and that mattered. At least, it mattered to him.

"We don't have to do this," he said, his voice more annoyed than he intended it to be. "If you don't want to."

Her brow furrowed. "You're defensive," she said. Like it was a fact. Because it was. "Why are you defensive?" She tilted her head to the side and gave him a pointed stare. "This doesn't have to mean anything. Sex is sex. I know guys like to think that girls can't separate sex and love but we can. At least, I can." She narrowed her eyes when she saw him smirk. "What?"

"You're babbling," he said, cocking his head to the side and looking at her with a knowing glint, even through the haze of lust. "You're nervous. Which means this isn't just about sex to you. It's more."

She felt her cheeks start to heat up. "Is it," she began.

"You're cute when you're nervous," he said, interrupting her without a care in the world. He reached out and curled a strand of hair around his finger. "Especially if I'm the one making you nervous."

"Do you want sex to mean more to you?" she forced herself to ask, forced herself to not think about his words and the effect they were having on her heart.

He stared at her for a long moment. "You really don't get it, do you?" he asked. "What you do to me." He shook his head, the corner of his lips tilted up. "I want what you want, Harp. I want you. I do. But sex isn't just sex to me. Not when it comes to you."

Harper swallowed, nodding her head. She had no idea why she was nodding her head. Probably because she didn't know what else to say.

"How do you feel?" he asked, his eyes still intense, still cloudy and dark.

"I," she said, "I don't know how I feel, to be honest. I just know I want you." She locked eyes with him, the truth of her words surprising even her. "I want you."

His nostrils flared at her words, his gaze becoming even more intense, and he nodded his head. He didn't hesitate and took her in his arms before claiming her lips like they were his, like he had any right to claim them at all. She opened willingly to him, and when he started to tug at her shirt, she didn't pull away, didn't stop him.

Because she did want him.

Badly.

It wasn't long before her shirt and bra had been carelessly discarded on the floor, Zach on top of Harper, her back on the bed, his mouth devouring every inch of skin she could offer him. Her legs were already wrapped around him and her impatient fingers tugged on his shirt so she could see his skin, feel his body flesh to flesh.

When it was finally off him and disposed of, she let her fingers roam every ripple of his muscles. She reveled in the way he twitched under her touch, loved the way someone as strong as he was became powerless under her fingers. He was tight in all the right places, and a part of her wished she had a better view of his back because she was positive she would find the muscles there just as strong as his chest, if not more so.

"You're beautiful," she breathed out, not being able to contain the words any longer. Her eyes found his as her words compelled him to stop kissing her. Instead, he simply stared, like he was in shock. Like he had no idea what to say to that.

"No one's ever said that to me before," he murmured. It wasn't something he should have told her, but she was glad for it anyway.

"Then everyone who came before was fools," she said.

At that moment, he sprung on her. Passion sizzled between them, her fingers clawing at his arms, his back, anywhere she touched. It wasn't long before the rest of their clothes were shed and they were completely bare for the other, on complete display.

"You're beautiful, Harper" he said. It was cliché, she knew, and she had just told him the same thing, but the way he looked at her when he said it, the fact that he said her name... To her, there was meaning behind the words other than mere flattery. He meant them.

She kissed him in response. She could feel the length of him press into the inside of her thigh, and her pelvis throbbed with moisture at the simple feeling of it.

In expert time, Zach managed to grab a condom, remove it from its wrapper, and sheath himself up in one moment. He didn't ask her if she was sure. He didn't tell her they didn't have to do this again. He took his time entering her, but he entered her with pride, without worry for himself or from her.

She gasped in response, needing a moment to get used to his girth, but then it was like riding a bike. A new, big bike.

Zach didn't go slow. Nor was he rough. But he couldn't seem to control himself when he was inside her. She knew she wouldn't come from this position, and she refused to have sex with Zach without coming, so she reached between them and started to massage her clit in the way only she knew how.

Zach seemed surprised by this, but he grunted in approval, his eyes getting even darker than she thought possible.

It wasn't long before she reached her peak. Her heart jumped in her throat and the only sound she heard was the pounding of her heart, somehow beating in time with Zach's thrusting. And then, like he knew, he whispered her name, and she was gone. She splintered around him in a million pieces with no desire to be put back together again. Zach wasn't far behind, and when he spilled himself inside of her, she felt this odd sensation of being whole, of being complete.

Harper hadn't planned on it, but she fell asleep with Zach inside her.

Chapter 15

ZACH WOKE Harper up by slowly caressing her nipples. She couldn't have been asleep for more than two hours, but it would seem Zach was up and ready to go. One look into his midnight blue eyes and she already felt herself moisten between her thighs. The look was pointed and predatory, like she was his prey and he was going to feast on her.

Except Harper wanted to be in control now. She wanted to be the one who called the shots. She wanted to make this strong, tough hockey player beg for more, moan her name, and be completely and utterly helpless.

As such, she pushed him so he was flat on his back. At first, he seemed surprised. His eyes widened and he opened his mouth to protest. But when she reached to his nightstand and grabbed a condom, he closed his mouth. There was still a hint of wariness in those eyes, but he was hard against her thigh and it would appear that he trusted her enough to see where she planned to take this.

Harper smirked as she opened the condom and slowly slid the slick material onto his cock. She drew it out, using one hand to put it on and the second to idly play with his balls. He hissed at the contact, but pleasure clouded his eyes. He was sensitive there, she realized, just like every man she'd been with. Probably just like every man.

Without warning, she straddled him and slid down his considerable length. She should have been accustomed to his size already, since they had had sex so recently, but she had to slow her ministrations down just to allow herself some time to stretch around him. He groaned in response and held onto her waist, helping her ease down.

"Fuck, you're already wet," he muttered, his eyes squeezed shut. His grip on her was firm.

"Can you imagine what I would feel like without the condom?" she asked before she could stop herself.

His eyes flashed open, capturing hers. "Don't tempt me, Harper," he said, and she felt a shock to her pelvis at the way he said her name.

She grinned down at him and started to roll her hips on top of him, the same way she had danced last night, early this morning, she couldn't keep track. Any retort that was ready to come out of his perfect mouth was snuffed out the minute she started to move, and even she was cast under a spell, his cock impaling her in just the right spot. She should speed up, but she couldn't. She was forced to go slow.

His hands cupped her breasts, his long thumbs caressing her nipples in just the right way that was firm but gentle, eliciting a throb of pleasure to soak the thrusting his cock was already doing to her. She threw her head back, her eyes rolling closed as her left hand found her clit and she started dancing along the swollen nub, begging for release.

Orgasm came easy, hard and slow. It was different, coming slowly. It was powerful and shook her to her core. It was hard to grasp it the way she did coming hard and fast, but this orgasm lasted longer and the waves rolled consistently until she couldn't touch herself anymore. Until she was too sensitive for Zach's fingers on her nipples. She had to push them away.

"You're amazing," he murmured through hooded eyes. She watched as he gave her a lazy smile, those dark blue eyes never leaving hers. She felt shy under his gaze, which was silly, considering what they had just done again, but she did not look away from him, nor did she immediately get off. He softened inside of her but she liked the way he felt inside her, the way her body felt with him. It wasn't like the way she had been with the guys who came before Zach.

It was different.

She refused to think about it.

"I should get to my room," she murmured, prepared to slide off him and grab her underwear so she didn't make too much of a mess. Zach's hands immediately stopped caressing her hips, and instead, gripped them with just enough pressure to keep her in place.

"Don't go just yet," he said, and pulled her down so she was lying on top of him. "Hang out for just a little bit longer."

She should go. Harper knew she should go. Who knew when Zach's roommate would be back and it was already bad enough that they saw her and Zach together at the club. She didn't want to be known as a puck bunny and a part of her worried that any respect she had from them when she first introduced herself was thrown out the window.

Surprisingly enough, Harper didn't regret what happened between
her and Zach. Truth be told, she thought she would. She thought she would worry about their relationship, her job, and how the team perceived her. And she did. To a degree. But not enough to wish she hadn't agreed to go out with him tonight, to kiss him the way she had at the club, and to be with him in his bed.

She wouldn't necessarily say they made love, but she also didn't think they fucked. It was an in-between that had the roughness and the intimacy of both. She liked it, she realized. In fact, Harper would never admit it out loud, but she could get used to it.

With him.

So she agreed. She let her body relax. She let her eyes close. And she allowed herself to fall asleep in surprisingly comfortable arms.

HARPER AWOKE to the comfortable pressure between her legs. She hadn't been drunk when Zach kissed her. She hadn't been tired or tipsy when they went back to the hotel room together. She was completely sober when she heard the rip of the plastic, when she felt his considerable length enter her body. She didn't even try to stop it. She didn't want to.

And now. Now.

Her eyes dropped to Zach. He slept on his stomach, his face away from hers, but one arm still thrown carelessly across her stomach, his fingers sprawled out like she was his, like he was afraid she would slink off into the night.

Her heart felt full at the thought, but the fear immediately jumped in. She had wanted it, wanted him. Badly. She was surprised at how badly she wanted him. Maybe it was because she hadn't been with anyone since Bryan and wanted to know that someone desired her in that way. And yeah, there was an element of pride that went along with bedding a hockey player. But now, those feelings, that pride, didn't mean much to her. Any hope of deepening the relationship on an emotional level probably went completely out the window. Her chest ached, but she pushed it aside.

Never again. She couldn't let this happen again. Any respect he had for her probably vanished. Not that she cared what he thought of her –

No. That was a lie. Harper hated to admit it, but she did care what he thought about her. Because despite his many personality flaws, Harper truly believed that Zach was a good guy.

She had to get out of there. She would sneak out and pretend this never happened. She pointedly ignored when her heart squeezed in response to the decision she made. Her first goal was to get out of Zach's grasp without him knowing. Then, she would go back to her room, go to the game, and fly home early – even if she had to pay for it out of her own pocket. Then, she would tell Seraphina everything. Seraphina had created this position for her; the least Harper could do was treat her job seriously and give her boss respect.

Harper took a breath and sucked in her stomach. From there, she slowly began to edge her way to the end of the bed. Her eyes darted between the floor – so she wouldn't topple off with no warning – and Zach, to see if he would wake up. By the time her leg was able to drop to the floor, Zach still hadn't awoken. Twisting her body to stand up would be easy. She held her breath, angled her body, and stood in one fluid motion. Immediately, she held her breath and waited. But Zach continued snoring softly, didn't even move besides the even rise and fall of his chest from breathing.

A twinge of guilt hit her hard and unexpectedly. She chewed her bottom lip as she cast one last look at her lover, over his beautiful body. Memories flashed of last night and this morning. It was good. No, not good. The best she ever had. And she was going to give that all up.

She had to.

Harper shook her head. She needed to focus. She needed to get her head on straight.

It didn't take her long to pull on her bra and underwear. Instead of slinking on her dress, she grabbed his shirt and decided that it was long enough that it could pass off as a dress. If she ran into anyone, they would probably assume she had shorts on underneath the hemline of the shirt because no one in their right mind would walk around with just a shirt and high heels on.

The shoes were a problem. They definitely gave off a walk-of-shame vibe – and that was what she had been trying to avoid which was why she refused to wear her dress. There was nothing she could do unless she chose to go barefoot. She wasn't sure what was more damning. In the end, she supposed it didn't matter. As long as she left now, as long as he didn't see her leaving, that was all she cared about.

So she quickly ran her fingers through her hair, grabbed her shoes and her purse in her hands, and left Zachary Ryan sleeping in that bed without looking back. Even though she wasn't spotted as she made her long trek back to her room, she kept her chin up the entire time.

ZACH FELT her leave the minute she slipped from his grasp and got off the bed. He didn't want her to know he was awake, however. He hadn't particularly cared if a girl snuck off in the morning after a passionate night of lovemaking. Most of the time, he was sleeping when it happened. Sometimes they left notes, most of the times it was their number, but he rarely called them back. He wasn't looking for anything serious.

But Harper was different. He didn't want to see her leave. Because then, it was real. Then, it was over.

And, he realized to himself, the last thing he wanted was for it to be over.

Chapter 16

IT WAS two weeks since they had sex and a few days before opening game. Zach called Harper a couple of times but she didn't call him back. She had no idea what she was supposed to say or how she was going to communicate her feelings – feelings she didn't even understand. Harper didn't want to lead Zach on, nor did she want to waste her time. After everything that had happened between her and Bryan, it was hard for her to open up again. In fact, if she was being honest, it was one of the last things she wanted to do.

Which was terrible, because she knew she liked Zach. A lot. She knew there was a spark there, something that set Zach apart from the rest but she didn't know if she was ready to take that step yet, to trust someone new.

It was frustrating because the desire was there – the desire for him and to let him in, but she couldn't bring herself to do so. Not yet, anyway. So she acted like a coward. She avoided the situation because nobody got hurt.

Harper knew she was throwing something good away by not taking a chance and she hated herself for it. But she didn't want to get tangled up with someone new when she needed to sort herself out. If she was still afraid of her last boyfriend, she couldn't possibly be ready for a new one. It wasn't fair to Zach and it wasn't fair to herself.

The stress must have caught up with her because by the time late September rolled around, she came down with a bad cold. Her nose was clogged up so badly that she found herself waking up in the middle of the night because she couldn't breathe. She also refused to take saline drips because she didn't want to get addicted to them. Because of the sinus issue, her head swelled up and she had constant headaches. She was pretty sure her eyes were red, her skin was pale – which washed out her face and made her freckles look darker than they were – and her hair was limp and lifeless and also probably oily due to the fact that she hadn't washed it.

When Monday morning rolled in, Harper called Seraphina to let her know she wouldn't be in. Her voice was raw and scratchy, which, while felt like gargling glass, made Harper feel as though she wasn't lying.

When that was finished, she headed over to her couch, grabbed her Roku control, and flipped to Netflix. She never really had an opportunity to indulge in some binge watching and she wanted to get more into *Grey's Anatomy*. She had cranberry juice and popcorn on the coffee table, her favorite quilt wrapped around her body, and her bedroom pillow on the arm of the couch, so she could lie down comfortably.

Three and a half episodes in, there was an unfamiliar knock on the door. Harper's eyes flitted over to the door, and she debated on whether or not she was actually required to answer it. Her grandmother would have called beforehand to make sure she was home before dropping by and she would know Bryan's knock regardless of the amount of time spent apart. Not in a romantic way, but because the sound of him unnerved her, set her on edge. It was as though her body was protecting her from any potential threat he posed to her.

After crossing both of them off, she couldn't help but be

intrigued on who would be visiting her without giving her any kind of notice. The stranger knocked again, more insistently, and then a familiar voice called out: "The soup's getting cold!"

Zach.

Zach was outside her door. With soup, apparently.

Harper's heart fluttered in her chest and she nearly tripped over herself before rushing to the door. Her congested head made her light on her feet as the blood rushed to accommodate the jerky movement she was making, but she managed to right herself as she reached for the handle. As she opened the door, her mind screamed at her about looking terrible and how she didn't want to get Zach sick before the start of the season, but her heart forced her to open the door, if only to see him again.

Her heart skipped twice when he shot her a warm smile and she couldn't help but notice as his blue eyes softened when they saw her.

"You look terrible," he told her as he walked through the door without any sort of invitation. Almost like he owned the place.

She huffed in response, immediately closing the door and locking it, before spinning around on the ball of her foot so she could keep up with him. Somehow, Zach knew exactly where to go to set down two bags of Boudin on her dining table before taking a seat himself.

"What are you doing here?" Harper asked, standing behind an empty seat and placing her hands on the back of the chair to keep her balance. "You can't just walk in here."

"Seraphina said you were sick," he said as he began to remove the contents of the brown paper bags and put them on the table. "Do you want to use your bowls? Well, I got bread bowls so I guess that question doesn't matter."

"Seraphina told you I was sick?" she asked, furrowing her brow together.

"You know you sound sexy with your raspy voice," he said

with a smirk. "The fact that you're rubbing your nose every five seconds just adds to the seduction."

"There is no seduction!" she exclaimed, her fingers balled into fists as she stomped her foot. She felt especially juvenile right now. "And you didn't answer my question. There is no way Seraphina would walk up to you and tell you that I was sick."

"I asked where you were," he told her with a shrug. "Question: are you cool with using plastic spoons? I can grab your spoons, if you'd prefer."

"Why on earth would you ask Seraphina?" Harper asked. Maybe it was the fact that her head was clogged or she was still attuned to *Grey's Anatomy*, but she still didn't understand how he found out she was sick.

"You weren't answering my calls," he said without looking at her. "I figured if you didn't want to see me anymore, the least you could do was tell me to my face."

"Zach," she said through a sigh. Her cheeks burned with shame, and she couldn't bring herself to look at him. As much as she hated to admit it, he was right. If she didn't want to see him anymore, she should have told him a long time ago. The problem was, she didn't know what she wanted, and she told him as much.

His brows furrowed. "That's bullshit and you know it," he said. "Now, please sit down. I don't want your soup getting cold. Have you had this New England Clam Chowder?"

Harper smiled despite herself and took a seat across from him. "It's my favorite," she murmured.

"Mine, too," Zach said.

It was silent for a long moment as the two ate their soups in silence. Harper loved the feeling of the hot food sliding down her throat. It still hurt to swallow but she craved the warmth it provided her, especially when she was sick on a particularly overcast day.

"Thank you," she finally said, when she was halfway

through the meal. It was hard to eat – her appetite not what it used to be before becoming ill – but she refused to let the soup go to waste. "And you're right about me not calling you. I should have done so. I'm sorry."

"I'm a big boy," Zach told her. "I can handle rejection. The thing is, I don't think you realize what you're rejecting. There's something between us, Harp, and it wasn't just sex – which was the best I've ever had, by the way. The date we went on, to the beach for breakfast, was one of the best days of my life."

Harper was surprised. She couldn't help it.

"And I know you had fun, too," Zach said, throwing a glance at her. "You can't fake that."

"I did enjoy myself," she admitted, resting her chin in her palm. "More than I expected."

"So why are you denying what's here?" he asked. "I don't understand why you wouldn't want to take this chance on something I know I've never felt before." He paused to take a sip of the soda he brought with him.

"Honestly, I have no idea what this is," she told him, her eyes bright with honesty. "I don't know what I feel or what I'm going to feel or anything. My past has left me... wounded. It's hard for me to open up."

Zach gave her a look. "I'm sorry, but, again, that's bullshit," he told her. "You're overthinking something that should come to you so simply. You like me. I know it. Don't be in denial about it, with me or with yourself. Just admit it. Admit it."

"Okay," Harper said, her brow furrowed in frustration. "Okay, you're right. I like you. I like you!"

"Whoa, no need to be crazy about it," Zach teased. "I like you, too."

Harper let out a breath she didn't realize she had been holding. He liked her. He said it out loud. It was real.

"So let's do something about it," he said, his voice softer, gentler. His hands held her forearms and they were firm but caressing at the same time. Like he was aware of his own strength and was controlling it. "I know this talk is supposed to come before sex traditionally. Whether I actually adhere to what proper etiquette says is another story but I want to give it a shot with you. Because I like you. A lot. And this isn't because the sex was great."

Harper felt herself smile. "You already said that," she pointed out.

"I can't help it if it's the truth," he told her. His blue eyes sparkled with earnest. "I want to see where this goes. I want to be around you. I'm not saying we have to get married and pop out a bunch of kids, but I'd at least like the opportunity to get to know you better. And for you to get to know me."

Harper felt herself smile. "You're right," she said. "I do like you. I want to see where this goes." She looked down at her half-eaten bread bowl. "I'm sorry I didn't respond to your calls. That was chicken shit of me."

"It was," he agreed. "Luckily for you, I'm a forgiving person, as I'm sure you'll find out soon enough."

She laughed and he leaned in and gave her a chaste kiss on her lips. She smacked his shoulder.

"What are you doing?" she exclaimed. "I can't have you getting sick. The season starts in a couple of weeks and we can't have you hacking up a lung when you need to start shooting the puck."

"Everyone's a critic," he muttered with a smile on her face. "By the way, you don't get to tell me I'm not allowed to kiss you. You're my girl now, and I'm going to kiss you whenever I want."

Harper grinned and gave him a quick peck on the cheek. "Now, finish your soup. I spent six ninety-nine on that and I don't want my good money to go to waste."

Harper laughed. Before she could dig back into her food, there was a knock on the door. She furrowed her brow, surprised she had another visitor, but went to answer it regardless. It was probably her grandmother. Harper hadn't been checking her phone and she wouldn't be surprised if her grandmother showed up to take care of her the way she had when Harper was young.

When Harper threw open the door, she was hit with the realization that it was not her grandmother.

Chapter 17

HARPER DIDN'T THINK TWICE about opening the front door. She should have known better. She was just having too much fun with Zach that she didn't even think to check the peephole.

There, on the other side of the door, was Bryan, and he looked nothing short of pissed. The minute her eyes rested on the familiar slump of his shoulders as he leaned on her doorstep, the way he rested his weight on his left leg, popping out his right hip, the way his brown hair constantly fell into his face, she reached for her door in order to close it. He was too quick, however, and he lifted up his left arm and prevented the door from closing.

"Wait, wait, wait, Harp," he said. "I wanted to talk to you about something" – he cut himself off as his eyes took in her appearance. Harper didn't care that she looked absolutely wretched. She didn't care that she was in a large plaid shirt and yoga pants or that her hair was frizzy and hadn't been washed in three days or that her face was dry, with dried snot just above her lips. However, Bryan looking at her at all, regardless of how she looked, was something that caused her skin to crawl. She hated when he looked at her, especially with longing. "You look sick."

"I am," she said quickly, pushing into the door to a close, "so I'll talk to you later. Don't want to get you sick."

Bryan maintained his grip on the door, pushing back against her. "Are you okay?" he asked. "Is there anything you need?"

"To be honest, Bryan, I want to be by myself," she replied. She didn't struggle against Bryan, knowing it would be futile. Instead, her mind started thinking about ways to get rid of him before Zach got out of the kitchen. Her eyes narrowed and it was easy to look pissed when she had a head full of snot. "What do you want, Bryan?"

"I need to talk to you about something important, Harp," he said, his tone snagging a rough edge with each word. His eyes narrowed and he used more of his strength to open the door even wider. Without warning, he placed a folded newspaper against her chest. "Are you dating Zachary Ryan?"

"What?" Harper asked, completely baffled. He dropped his hand and she caught the newspaper by clutching it to her chest as he pushed his way in, taking care not to physically touch Harper in any way. "Why would you even ask that?"

Bryan gave her a look – the same look that crawled underneath her skin years ago. It was condescending and infuriating and it made her feel like an idiot. Every time he used it on her, she had this irresistible urge to slap it off of his face.

"Don't play dumb, Harp," he said, his voice dry. "You know. I know. All of Arizona knows about you and Zach. There's photographic evidence. I didn't realize you were a puck slut, though. Maybe that's why we didn't work. Because I'm not a hockey player."

"We didn't work because you're a hypocritical asshole who can't take responsibility for his own actions," Harper said before she could stop herself. Her eyes widened when she finished, but she didn't regret saying what she had to say.

She was almost afraid to look at Bryan for his reaction.

Almost. But she stood her ground and she did not look away, even as his cold eyes flashed with anger, and he clenched his teeth together so hard that his jaw popped. She watched as he squeezed his long fingers into tight, white-knuckled fists and tried to contain his rage.

Harper swallowed, recognizing that reaction. Her entire body seized up, like it was prepared to take whatever punishment he was going to give her. But her eyes remained on him, despite the familiarity of his anger, despite her fear. She still had a long way to recovery, but this was something she had never been able to accomplish before.

"What did you say?" he asked in a tightly controlled voice.

Bryan was different, too. Usually, he would already be yelling at her or retaliating by calling her all sorts of terrible things. That might have meant something to her back when they were dating. Now, however, she didn't particularly care what sort of person he was and who he was becoming. She didn't care about him at all.

"Did she stutter?"

And there was Zach, pressed against her back, towering over her and offering any and all the protection she could ask for. She felt small standing by him, and somehow, stronger. Like he would be there for her, through the good times and the bad times.

Bryan didn't take his eyes off Harper. "So it's true," he said, his voice flat. "You are a puck slut."

Before Harper could even process what was happening, Zach took a step forward. In one fluid motion, he pushed her behind him as a way to shield her from Bryan's gaze and punched Bryan square in the face. Bryan grunted and his head snapped back. He almost hit his head smack on the wall behind him.

"Get up." Zach stalked over to him and pulled Bryan up by his shirt and forced him to stand on his two feet. "If you ever come back here, you ever try to contact Harper again, you'll have more problems than a black eye. I don't want you to even say her name. You are done. Do you get me?"

"*I'm* done?" Bryan asked, taking a step back, out of Zach's tight grip. "*I'm* done? You're a professional athlete and you just assaulted a member of the general public. *You're* done. You are going to be sorry. Both of you."

"Are you threatening me?" Zach asked, squaring his shoulders. Bryan had never been slight by any means, but standing next to Zach made him look small. It delighted Harper to see him be the smaller person in a tense situation. He couldn't use his size to intimidate her anymore.

Bryan did not flinch but Harper noticed his body tense as Zach took a step towards him. And then another.

"Get out," Zach repeated. He reached behind Zach and thrust open the door. He didn't push Bryan out but Harper knew Zach would do what was necessary to get Bryan out of the house. "Get out and don't come back."

Bryan looked to Harper, his eyes filled with more rage than she had ever seen before. He didn't have to tell her anything; she knew what he said. Bryan was going to make them pay for this, both of them, in whatever way he could. Maybe she could figure out how to get another restraining order and add Zach as a protected person.

When Bryan was finally gone, Zach closed and locked the door. He turned, his eyes still hard and cold, his body still rigid and tense. Harper bit her tongue. She wanted to apologize. She wanted to make Zach forget everything he went through because there was no way any sane person would want to be with her, with someone who had Bryan as baggage.

But then his eyes found her, and they softened, and before Harper realized what was happening, he swept her in his arms and pressed her against his chest. He started murmuring things in her hair, things she couldn't quite hear but at least understood the sentiment. She allowed herself to close her eyes and fall into his arms, and before she knew it, she could hear his heartbeat in his chest, against her ear. It was strong and steady, and the repetition caused her to relax and slowly drift off to sleep.

⊏══⊐

WHEN SHE WOKE UP, Harper couldn't tell if it was day or not. To be honest, she didn't particularly care. Zach's arms were around her waist and her head was on his chest and they were wrapped up in the sheets on her bed.

She felt herself smile at the sight of him, his head on her pillows, his dark blond hair messy and all over the place (somehow despite its shortness). She couldn't stop staring at him, at the way his nostrils flared as he softly snored, at the slight gap between his lips. He looked vulnerable, completely comfortable with her in her bed in her home. She was positive it wasn't the mansions he was used to since skyrocketing to NHL fame and she supposed that it endeared him to her even more. That regardless of the wealth he accumulated, he still looked natural in a small bedroom.

"You think too loud," Zach mumbled, keeping his eyes closed as though he were still sleeping. "I can feel you staring at me."

Harper felt her cheeks turn pink, but she smiled and said, "I like looking at pretty things."

Zach's lips turned up. "You think I'm pretty?" he asked, somewhat surprised.

"I wouldn't be with you if you weren't," she said. "You don't have a great personality."

Without warning, Zach flipped her on her back and proceeded to tickle her sides. Harper started laughing out loud, a bark of a laugh that shook her to the bones.

"Please," she managed to get out. "Stop!"

"I didn't know you were ticklish, Harper," Zach said as he continued his onslaught on her. "Why didn't you mention that to me? How dare you keep this integral piece of information from me! Do you think I'd use it against you like I'm doing right now?"

Harper tried wiggling out of his grip, but it was too tight. Her legs started pushing out and if Zach wasn't careful, she was going to kick him.

"Please," she managed to get out again.

"All right, all right," he said, "since you asked so nicely."

Harper smiled once he relented, and wrapped her arms around him as he pulled her closer to him. "Thank you," she said after a comfortable moment of silence. "For what you did with the whole Bryan thing. You shouldn't have had to see that."

"That's the thing, Harp," he murmured to her, eyes on her like she was a sunset or something else just as unique and glorious. "I want to see the messy bits of your past. I want to know all about you. That's what being in a relationship is all about."

"So we're in a relationship, then?" she asked, her lips turning up.

Zach nodded. "I thought you knew," he said. "But you shouldn't be embarrassed. Not about your past. I'm not going to judge you." He sat up slowly. "I would like to see that paper he gave you, though. I hadn't realized people had taken pictures of us."

"I didn't think people in Arizona would even know who you were," Harper murmured.

"Ouch," Zach said, pulling on his shirt. Harper watched his muscles ripple as he moved, and the simple white v-neck clung to his body like it was a second skin,

"You know what I mean," Harper said, standing.

"I don't, actually," he said. "Come on. Let's go check them out. I left the paper on the table before taking you to bed."

"Thanks for that, too," Harper murmured, suddenly shy.

"You don't have to thank me, Harper," he told her and kissed her cheek. "I would do anything for you."

Harper was silent because she wasn't sure how to respond. But she did know she believed him.

Chapter 18

"AT LEAST THEY caught me from my good side," Zach said as he looked at the pictures, his eyes roving over the sports section of The Phoenix Sun. "The real question is, how did Bryan even get these pictures?"

Harper felt her cheeks burst into flames as she shrugged her shoulders. She had never regretted much of anything in her life before, but being with Bryan was probably the only thing. She knew it made her learn about herself and she was grateful for the experience, but when push came to shove, she was embarrassed that someone like her could ever be with someone like him. Bryan was good looking, but he was weird, possessive and, when things got bad, abusive.

"I have no idea," she said and then pressed her lips together.

"Was he stalking you?" Zach asked, snapping his head to her. "I mean, from what you've told me about him, he would fall into that category."

"I don't know," Harper said, snapping even though that wasn't her intention. She pulled her eyes away from the newspaper and forced them to Zach's face. "I'm sorry. I just don't like talking about him. He's not even in my life anymore but he already brings out the worst in me."

Zach reached out to touch her. From her peripheral vision, she watched as he flexed his fingers in hesitation before pushing through it and placing his hand on her shoulder. "Tell me what happened," he said in a soft murmur. His blue eyes pooled with sincerity. "Tell me so I can be there for you."

Harper clenched her jaw, looking away. She wanted to tell Zach, wanted to let him in.

"Please."

It was the word that made her come undone.

"There's really nothing more to tell you than I already have," she said, staring at the table underneath her hands rather than at him. She didn't think she'd be able to talk if she had to look at him. "He wasn't always bad. In fact, the majority of the time, he was sweet. But every now and then…" She clenched her jaw but forced herself to continue. She needed to be able to get this out if she was ever going to move on. "He would critique the way I looked. One time, he told me the fact that my part was centered pissed him off. Like I can help that my hair naturally parts in the middle. He would always be on my case about looking a certain way if we went out. I get that maybe I should have put more effort into my appearance. I understand how important it is to try for your partner. I just didn't appreciate the fact that he was quick to cut me down and hard to get a compliment out of him.

"A lot of the times, I would call him out on the hypocrisy of his behavior. Normally, it would lead to a big fight because he would get mad at my reaction to something he said rather than realize if he hadn't said anything in the first place, I wouldn't be upset." Harper couldn't help but roll her eyes when she told him. "But he was terrible at taking responsibility for anything. Instead, he would blame me, blame my reactions to things, blame the way I handled stuff. So I said something about it. And we would fight. A lot. We both have bad tempers so it wasn't long before one of us was shouting and saying mean things and…" She shook her head. "Things got bad. And I think when you're in that, you don't see it. But when you get your space and you take the time to yourself, you see it from the outside.

"He left on a business trip and I got that realization pretty fast. So I made my decision that once he got back, I would break up with him. I refused to do it over the phone or through a text. I knew exactly what I was going to say and how I was going to say it.

"When he got home, he was just the sweetest guy. He treated me the same way he had in the beginning of our relationship, like nothing had changed. And I couldn't break up with him, not when it felt so wonderful to be around him.

"A couple of weeks later, we had our worst fight to date." She smiled to yourself. "I can't even remember what we were fighting about. Probably something stupid because our fights were pretty pointless. And without warning, he grabbed me by my arms, slammed me against the wall, and put his fingers around my throat. He choked me until I was clawing at his hands, begging him to let me go. I honestly thought he was going to kill me.

"When he dropped me to the floor, I ran to my bathroom, locked myself in, and called the cops. He tried to coax me out of there with apologies and compliments, but I couldn't bring myself to leave until the police came. I just kept thinking, 'If he hadn't stopped, I could have died' over and over again."

"You didn't flinch when I did that to you in bed," Zach pointed out in a low murmur. "If you had told me…"

Harper shook her head. "It's different," she said, placing her hand on his forearm. "You're different. I trust you."

Zach smiled but it didn't reach his eyes. His jaw was clenched and he couldn't help but stare at Harper, taking her in. She felt herself flush under his scrutiny and she looked away. He reached out, flexing his fingers until they brushed the flesh of her neck. She tensed but did not flinch, and the tension was not because she was afraid of him. No. It was because he was touching her. Goosebumps sprang up wherever he touched her, like a shadow trailing after its master.

"What happened next?" he managed to get out, his voice tight, controlled. It almost sounded like he was angry, like he had to know the conclusion even though he might not want to.

"The cops came," she breathed. She tried to ignore Bryan's fingers on her throat, but she couldn't seem to shake them off as easily as she thought she would. "Two of them. Both men. Very polite. I still remember their names. Lee and Lonigro. They got me an emergency protective order that night and they served him with it a little later. We went to court to get an extension after it expired and they granted it to me. It was active for a year, and in that year, I never heard from him. I never saw him. To be honest, I completely forgot about him.

"Until he showed up. He would never make contact with me, but I started noticing him at places I was, like the gym or the grocery store. I hadn't realized the restraining order expired. I kept telling myself I'd go renew it, but I kept putting it off and he never made direct contact so I thought that maybe it was just a coincidence..." She let her voice trail off, sighing as her eyes scanned the picture of her and Zach once again. "I thought it was over."

"It might not be over," Zach said, placing a hand on her shoulder, "but it's different. I will never let anyone hurt you again, Harper. I promise."

"Zach, I appreciate that, but it's not your responsibility to protect me." She craned her neck from her seat at the kitchen table so she could look him in the eyes. "I need to figure this out."

"*We* do," he corrected gently. He removed his hand from her shoulder only to slide into the chair next to her and take her hand in his. She hadn't realized how big his hand was, dwarfing hers entirely. He pressed his lips together, his eyes going over Harper's face, her neck, down to her collarbone, before looking up at her once again. "Did you hear what happened in Toronto?"

Harper shook her head. "No, not really," she murmured. "Just the rumors."

"What did you hear?"

Harper caught his eye, furrowing her brow. She didn't know why he wanted to talk about this now, but ever since the Gulls had acquired Zach, she had been curious about the validity of the rumors and how they affected his former team. Quite a lot, if Toronto was willing to trade him for so little.

"I heard that you slept with Brewer's wife," Harper said, "cheating on your girlfriend at the time." She forced her eyes into his. It was tough for her to maintain because she didn't want him to think she believed them and didn't want to come across like she was judging him if he had.

Zach nodded like that was what he expected.

"I didn't actually sleep with Tina," he said. His hands were flat on the surface of the table and he looked down at the veins on the back of his hands. "The team went out after a win last season to a local underground nightclub. I went because I liked hanging out with the guys. The thing people don't understand is, at least with me, I don't go to these clubs looking to get laid. I could give a shit about the girls. I just want to hang out with my team, drink a beer, and enjoy myself."

Harper found herself smiling, nodding her head. She looked the sound of Zach's voice, deep with a slight Toronto accent, where the 'o' sound was drawled out a little bit more.

"For some reason, the wives showed up. To this day, I don't know if the guys mentioned it to them or if they were actually invited, but they showed up and knew exactly where to find us. Of course, they were either at the bar or in their own group, dancing to the music. Yes, as hockey players especially in Canada, we get recognized a lot more than we do here in the

States, but for the majority of the players, they still believe in what marriage is. They don't cheat.

"I get that the wives sometimes feel abandoned and unappreciated. I get it. Especially if they don't work and have three kids and we're traveling, it's tough. I know a lot more wives that cheat much more than the players.

"Gordon Brewer wasn't even out that night. I have no idea why she came unless one of the wives told her what was going on and she wanted to come." He shrugged. "But she was there. Tina is pretty. Really, really pretty. Brewer takes her for granted. Everyone knows it. I didn't really know her but she seemed nice and if she put up with Brewer, she had some determination."

"Or she wanted the status of being married to a hockey player," Harper pointed out before she could stop herself.

Zach pushed his brow up. "That's an excellent point," he said. "Anyway, she was there and we started talking. I felt bad for her – she looked lonely and I didn't want her to feel awkward. So I started talking to her and one thing led to another and she was on my lap, kissing my neck. The guys were still dancing and they could have walked in at any moment. I pushed her off me. She was startled but nothing bad happened – like, she didn't get hurt or anything.

"She didn't take the rejection well. She started making up these lies, about how I hit on her and how I had sex with her in the room. I was afraid she was going to say I raped her, but she didn't. Only that I got her a strong drink and she wasn't able to say no. Almost as bad, I know. Dianne didn't believe me. She had accused me of cheating at least once a month, after a road trip. The guys completely ostracized me. I tried to explain but they didn't believe me and I stopped trying. I figure if they were so quick to believe her, I wasn't going to push it. Management found out, and when they offered me the trade, I jumped at it. I didn't even care where they sent me. I wound up here." His eyes dropped to her lips. "Little did I know, the worst thing that ever happened to me would be the best thing."

He leaned over and kissed her. "How are you feeling?" he asked.

"Better," she said.

He nodded. "Good," he said, "because I want you. I think we've done enough talking for one day." His lips curled up in a mischievous grin. "Let's break in your couch."

Chapter 19

HARPER DIDN'T SLINK out of bed the next morning. She allowed herself the privilege of remaining in his arms. She had never gotten a more restful sleep since she broke up with Bryan years ago. Somehow, Zach had this ability to make her feel safe. Protected. Like nothing bad could happen to her.

When he woke her up the next morning to make love to her again, she was more than willing to open her body up the way she opened up her soul to him last night. She had no idea how it was possible, but somehow, once she was vulnerable and completely honest with Zach – and herself – about everything, sex was enhanced. Better than before, which was saying something.

"I have practice this morning," he murmured into her hair as he pulled her against him so he could kiss her shoulder blade. "Maybe I should call in sick and blame you."

"Stop it," Harper said with a soft smile on her face. Her eyes were closed and she breathed in a deep, clear breath. She felt at peace, content, like all was right in the world. "You need to go to practice, especially after that last game where you had a wide open net and somehow still decided to pass it."

He laughed and she found that she loved the sound of it. She wanted to make him laugh even more.

"You're starting to sound like Cherney," he told her. "Good thing I have a thing for bald women with thick mustaches."

Now, it was Harper who laughed. She wiggled around in his arms so she could look him in the eye. "I'm being serious," she told him. "I don't want to be that girl who holds you back. I know the team comes first" –

"You come first," he corrected, "in more ways than one." He kissed the point of her nose. "But I appreciate it. I know what you mean."

"You know I'm serious, though, right?" Harper asked. Zach furrowed his brow and opened his eyes but kept his mouth closed, waiting for her to go on. "I know girls say things and do things differently. I get that. I just want you to know that when it comes to this, I completely understand. I *want* you to put the team first. I respect how hard you've been working and I wouldn't let you throw it away for anything else. I think the only exception to that is if I were having your baby, and" – she stopped. "Okay, too soon. I promise I haven't been thinking about that." She closed her eyes, feeling herself turn red. "*Shit.*"

Zach chuckled, gripping her to him even tighter. "You're so cute when you babble, sweetie," he told her.

"Sweetie?" She quirked a brow and popped open an eye, looking at him with doubt.

"I happen to like pet names, thank you very much," he told her. "It's what I do when I'm serious about someone."

This caused Harper to grin. "You're serious about me?" she asked.

"As serious as a heart attack," he informed her. He gave her a lopsided smile and she couldn't help but smile in return. A genuine, warm smile.

"Stop it," she said, playfully slapping him on his bare chest. "Don't you have to get to practice?"

"I can call in," he told her. "I think I'm coming down with something. I think you got me sick."

She laughed again. "Go!" she said, thrusting her finger at the door. "I have to be there to write about it and there's no way I'm going to be nice if you don't show up."

He gave her a quick kiss on the lips. "That's fine with me," he said. "I like it when you're bad."

━━━

HARPER AND ZACH arrived at the Ice Palace in two separate cars within fifteen minutes of each other. Even though Zach did say he was serious about her, implying he wanted them to actually have a relationship rather than just some fun, Harper wasn't quite ready to publicize their new thing. She didn't think it would be professional in any capacity, and after a few weeks of feeling this out and making sure this was what she wanted, she planned to tell Seraphina everything first.

Harper tried to ignore the flutter of her heart as she stepped through the Palace doors and headed to take the elevator up to the club level of the rink. She hugged her notebook to her chest, her pen already between her fingers, and she tried to calm her anticipation down at seeing Zach again. Which was just silly, since she had seen him twenty minutes ago and they planned to meet up again for lunch.

Once the elevator reached the club level, the doors sprung open and she stepped out into a long hallway. There were a couple of boxes open during practice for the media to sit and watch. Some players had their family members there, while others preferred complete solitude. The players hadn't yet gotten to the recently swept ice, and as Harper slid into the first row of the box seats, she took in the gleaming ice.

The Ice Palace had a luxurious club level, with rare photographs of the team since its inaugural season in 1993 framed and placed along the off-white hallways. There was a goosebump-inducing black and white photograph of Dimitri Petrov looking at his wife after losing Game 5 in the Stanley Cup Finals. His wife was off-camera but everyone knew he was staring at her, face ashen, eyes wide and sad. To be honest, Harper wasn't sure how Dimitri felt being immortalized on the wall in this way, considering it was a loss and he was currently going through a divorce, but the photo was nothing short of haunting.

Similar photos littered the hallway, including one of Seraphina and Katella with their grandfather. Seraphina was no more than four, which made Katella six. Both girls looked strikingly similar to the way they look now – Seraphina with her blonde hair and big forest green eyes, Katella with her gold hair and sea-green eyes. Their personalities shone through – Katella's easy confidence and intelligence in how to hold her body; Seraphina's perceptive gaze and mischievousness.

Ken stood behind them, each hand on one shoulder of each granddaughter. He wasn't smiling, save for the fact that his lips were turned up, and he was staring at the camera with a protective glint in his periwinkle blue eyes. He wore a white golf shirt with the Gulls' anchor on the right breast pocket and tan slacks.

Harper didn't know much about the personal life of the founder and his family, but she did know Ken raised his granddaughters like they were his own after their parents died in a car crash. And for Seraphina to have found her grandfather murdered in his office… Harper couldn't even imagine what the sisters had gone through, what they were still going through as they carried on his legacy.

"What do you think so far?" Harry Burns asked, coming to sit by Harper in the box seat, cocking his head to the side. "Ryan's not a bad fit with Underwood."

Harper nodded. "You know what, Burns?" she said. "Surprisingly enough, I agree with you. The exhibition games have really showed how talented the guy is, if a little cocky."

Burns nodded. "I think it's just a good thing he finally got away from the scandal back in Toronto," he said. "I don't know if the guys will trust him alone with their wives anytime soon, but God, the guy is one hell of a player."

Harper bit her tongue to keep from making a smart retort. Burns didn't know the story and Zach wasn't planning on sharing it anytime soon. She could respect that, and she definitely wouldn't reveal that to the world. It didn't stop her blood from heating at the judgment, didn't stop her teeth from clamping down together to keep a smart retort from jumping out of her mouth.

"He is," she forced out.

She turned back to her notebook and opened it, tilting her head down so a curtain of hair prevented him from seeing her face. Harper didn't want to talk to him anymore; in fact, she wanted to focus on practice, on what she was going to write for the blog. She needed to make sure she didn't gush about Zach, especially now that they were together, but she didn't want to leave him out either, when he was an integral part of the new team.

It wasn't long before the buzzer blew overhead and the players started skating out in their practice jerseys. Each line had a specific color. Because Zach was on the first line, he, Underwood, and Alec Schumacher wore red. The second line wore orange, the third line wore green, and the fourth line wore blue.

Zach didn't even look at the media, didn't even acknowledge Harper with a casual look or a secret smile. He spoke to Underwood and Schumacher, and judging by the way they were laughing, it seemed like the three were already close friends. Harper felt herself smile. That was great. If they could develop a chemistry between them that extended in their personal life, the line would be unstoppable.

Currently, the players were all lined up at the blue line. One of Cherney's assistant coaches, Soto, was explaining a passing drill. Brandon Thorpe, all decked out in his goalie gear, was currently in net. His backup, Jimmy Stafford was just off to the side.

"What the hell are the police doing here?" Burns muttered from beside Harper.

Harper immediately turned to look. Sure enough, two uniformed police officers headed to rink with Seraphina in between them, a disgruntled look on her pretty face. She looked like she was trying to explain something to them, but by the stoic looks on their faces, they were either ignoring her and didn't care what she had to say.

Something sunk in Harper's gut as they made their way to the rink. Seraphina pushed on the metal level and opened the side door to the ice before leaning inside and trying to get Cherney's attention. Cherney immediately skated over to Seraphina and tilted his head down so he could talk to her. When Seraphina finished, Cherney turned to look at his players.

Harper's heart stopped. She knew what was going to happen before it did. Sure enough, Cherney skated over to Zach and whispered something to him. Zach furrowed his brow, confused. She could read his emotions clearly on his face as though she were right there on the ice with him. And she wished she was.

Zach glided over to where the police were and he started talking to them as he stepped off the ice. The media started muttering under their breaths. Some even whipped out their phones to start recording. Harper watched as Zach pressed his lips together in a grim line as he listened to one of the men speak to him. He didn't look happy.

And then, Zach slid his eyes over to Harper. There it was. The tell. Somehow, this was tied to what happened last night with Bryan. Bryan had gotten the cops involved and now Zach was being arrested. Seraphina was running her fingers through her hair. Cherney continued on with practice. And the media was having a field day.

Harper sunk into her seat, keeping her eyes to herself. She needed to find a way to help Zach.

Chapter 20

HARPER COULDN'T SLEEP that night. She stayed up, pacing her apartment, her hands either clutched behind her back or yanking at her hair. She needed to stop or she would pull out a chunk of her scalp. She couldn't think logically anymore. She couldn't sit down and write her article without Zach's face flashing in her head. She knew a little bit about the law and knew there wasn't sufficient evidence that she knew of keep him in jail. He would have the opportunity to bail out, but the hours passed and he still hadn't shown.

She was going to kill Bryan. How dare he go to the police! She was going to go down to the police department herself to issue a statement about how Zach was simply defending her but stopped. She didn't want to make it worse, and she had a job and the team to think about. Zach could afford a good lawyer, he could afford bail, he could…

She shook her head. She wished she had friends she could to talk to about this. Harper was tempted to call her grandmother, but she knew the old woman would go on a tirade about how awful Bryan was, and she didn't particularly want to talk about

Bryan right now when the mere thought of him infuriated her to no end.

Harper knew he was bad news. She knew he was trouble. She just didn't think he would ever do something as crazy as this. Which was stupid on her part. She should have known better.

And Zach... She hoped Zach would still want to be with her, but that was a stretch now, considering. And she couldn't blame him. Why the hell would he want to be with a girl whose ex literally got into a physical altercation with him and then got him arrested for assault? Probably not any sane person, that much she knew for sure. Which meant this new, fragile beautiful thing she had with Zach could be threatened because of a stupid choice she made when she was younger.

Maybe she could fix this. She had no idea how, exactly, but maybe there was something she could do to get Bryan to change his mind and drop the charges. Maybe there was a detective assigned to the case she could give her statement to.

She hated not being able to do anything. She felt helpless, and while pacing helped her burn some calories, it did nothing for her nerves.

At that moment, there was a knock on her door. She jumped at the sound of it, hoping, praying that it was Zach. She all but dashed to the door and sprung up on her toes in order to look out of the peephole.

Bryan.

Harper frowned. Definitely not who she expected to see. But maybe this was a good thing. She took a breath and opened the door. She would not cower when she saw Bryan face to face. She would not be afraid. She would demand he drop the charges and then get out of her life, once and for all.

"Yes?" she asked. Her entire body was tense – not because she was afraid but because she wanted to brace herself in case he attempted to push through the door as he had before.

"Is that how you greet an old friend?" he asked, cocking his head to the side and giving her what had once been a charming smile. Before he choked her. Before he had Zach arrested.

"No." She paused, waiting for him to say something. Her eyes burned with frustration, anger, and she felt those emotions that she used to be so afraid of gave her confidence and faith in herself. She felt stronger simply by experiencing these emotions and not backing down.

Harper wouldn't lie. She was still afraid of Bryan. There was a small part of her that might always be afraid of him. But that part was small and ignorant. This new woman used that fear as a strength rather than a weakness.

Bryan gave her a flat look. "We should talk," he said.

Harper pushed her brows up. "I agree," she said with a nod of her head. "So talk."

"Aren't you going to invite me in?" he asked.

"No."

He clenched his jaw. "I would prefer not to talk about this in public," he told her. "You're lucky I'm even talking to you at all. I could just walk away, let the law implement its justice." He turned his head so Harper had a clear view of the black eye on Bryan's face and she bit back a smile.

"Oh, please, Bryan," she said. "You know one of my friends works for Newport PD, right?" She looked at him like he was a moron. Which he was. "What happened after what you did to me? Even though I had bruises on my neck from when you choked me, did charges ever get filed? Or did they drop charges because there was insufficient evidence against you, despite the bruises on my face? The only good that came out of it was the restraining order."

"That expired, by the way," he said.

"Something I'm going to remedy very soon," she said through gritted teeth.

"Actually," Bryan said, extending his pointer finger, "I don't think you want to do that anytime soon. You want me to drop the charges? I have a deal for you."

"Why would I want to take you up on a deal when charges are going to get dropped anyway?" Harper asked.

"Are you absolutely sure they will?" Bryan asked, tapping his chin and tilting his head to the side. "Are you sure his case won't get sent to the young, hotshot LA fan, looking to throw the book at some Newport Beach hockey player in order to prove a point about violence in athletic settings – even on a professional level – and make a name for himself? Can you really guarantee that?"

Harper clenched her teeth together. Her heartbeat echoed in her ears. She couldn't guarantee that this wouldn't go to trial. Yes, Zach would bail out. But that didn't mean he wouldn't go to trial. It didn't mean the young, hotshot assistant district attorney wouldn't push for more investigation. That could bring up stuff Zach didn't want to get out, stuff about what happened in Toronto. It would put his family drama in the spotlight. It would ridicule Seraphina – again – for taking a chance on a problem player. The team itself would be ridiculed, perhaps even the sport due to its violent nature.

As much as she hated to admit it, Bryan was right. She couldn't guarantee anything.

"What do you want?" she all but spat. Her eyes were still burning, and there was a part of her – a small part of her – that hated him. It was the same size as the part of her that feared him, and even though the majority of her was indifferent to Bryan, the part that hated him was at the forefront of her body right now, taking over her emotions and causing her temper to flare.

He smirked because he knew he had her. She wanted nothing more than to slap that smirk off of his face. Her fingers twitched and she had to shove them behind her back in order to keep herself from actually indulging in temptation.

"I want to be given the opportunity to start over," he told her, his voice as smooth as silk. It didn't seem that he cared about their past, about the effect he had on her now and how his actions caused life-long repercussions. Because Bryan didn't care about her or her feelings for him. As long as they were together, that was all he cared about. "I want us to reconnect. I want us to have a second chance."

"That will never happen," Harper told him. "You said it yourself: I'm with Zach."

Bryan flicked his wrist dismissively. "Trivial matters that can be rectified with time, patience, and forgiveness," he told her. "Maybe you've shared a couple of dates with the guy, but you and I have a history. That counts for something."

"Not when the history between us is filled with yelling, fighting, and abuse," Harper pointed out.

"I didn't abuse you," Bryan snapped, his entire body contorting into a defensive hunch. "I lost control of myself. It was a mistake, a mistake that will never happen again."

"That's what they all say," Harper quipped before she could stop herself.

Bryan narrowed his eyes. "I don't have to give you this chance," he pointed out. "Zach can rot in the courtroom for all I care. You think I don't know he's going to bail out? Of course I know that. I'm not an idiot. He'll be out for a few weeks until the prosecutor pushes for a quick court date and he's forced to go to trial. Then, they'll bring in character witnesses. You know what those are, right? They portray him a certain way. You know the first place they'll go, right? Everything and everybody will be dragged in the mud. But you can prevent that."

Harper looked at him skeptically. "So all I would need to do is go on one date with you?" she asked. "I don't have to be with you. I don't have to go on a second date. Just one date?"

Harper didn't want to agree. She wanted to be far away from him at all costs. But she knew that what he told her still had some truth sprinkled in. It wouldn't surprise her if they tracked down Gordon Brewer's wife and she spewed her lies on the stand, despite being under oath, just to get back at his rejection.

Bryan nodded. "I can't guarantee you that there won't be more than that, should your old feelings start to resurface," he said. "But yes. I will drop all charges if you agree to go on one date with me."

Harper clenched his jaw. "Once the charges get dropped," she said finally, "I will agree to one date mid-afternoon in a public place."

"One date at night where you have to dress up," Bryan pushed, "and then I'll drop the charges."

Harper shook her head. "Charges get dropped first," she insisted. "You don't think I know that it's at the DA's discretion whether or not they prosecute a case? What happens if you go ask for the charges to be dropped, and your friend, the hotshot ADA refuses to drop them? You make good on your word and I'll go on a date with you."

"At night," Bryan put in.

Harper's nostrils flared. "At night," she agreed, though she did not want to. "I will dress up."

He stuck out his hand. "You have a deal," he told her. "Expect a phone call in the next couple of days."

Harper dropped her gaze to Bryan's outstretched hand before looking back at his face. There was no way in hell she was going to touch him in any capacity, not even to make their deal official.

He dropped his hand when he finally realized she wasn't going to shake it and nodded his head. "I'll see you soon, Harper," he murmured as he turned around to leave. "Very, very soon."

Harper all but slammed the door shut, taking extra care to lock it. She leaned against it, sliding down until she was sitting on the floor. She pulled at the roots of her hair gently, but just enough to feel a pull of pain. She had no idea what she had gotten herself into, and she wasn't sure how to feel about it.

All that mattered was getting Zach out and keeping him there.

Chapter 21

ZACH SHOWED up at Harper's apartment well into the evening. It took a few hours to book him, and since Newport Beach didn't actually hold those they arrested unless they were stuck in a sober cell, he was transported to Orange County Sheriffs in Santa Ana. He was interrogated at Newport and the cops while firm were polite and cordial. He wasn't even arrested save for the transportation process. At county, he was booked, and once that was all over with, he was finally able to post bail, catch a cab, and get dropped off at the Ice Palace where he could pick up his car and meet with Seraphina.

"How did that go?" Harper asked, gently chewing on the tip of her thumbnail. She couldn't sit still while Zach was explaining everything so she paced up and down the the tiny living room that made up her apartment.

Zach, much to Harper's disbelief, was completely calm about the entire situation. He sat on the couch, leaning forward with his elbows on his knees, his wrists hanging between his legs. He had that lazy smile on his lips and the mischievous sparkle in his crystal blue eyes. She wanted to throttle him, to be honest. How could he be so calm? How could he be okay with all that went on, with everything that he had to go through?

"It went as well as expected," he said with a shrug. He looked up at her and leaned back, resting his ankle on his knee. "She was pretty pissed at the whole thing, but not because of me, because of Bryan and everything that went down."

"So," Harper said slowly, "she's not angry with you?"

"Of course not," he said with a crooked grin. "I didn't tell her your history with Bryan. I didn't think it was my place to say anything. But I did let her know he's been harassing you for a while and I just lost it. Seraphina was very supportive in every aspect."

Harper glanced at the hockey player sharply. "What's that supposed to mean?" she asked, quirking her brow.

"I'm not going to lie, Harp," Zach said, tracing circles on the inside of her wrist. It didn't even appear as though he was aware he was even doing it. "I told her about us. At least, I told her how I feel for you."

Harper felt her lips tug up but she managed to suppress it. For now. "And how is that?" she asked.

He grinned down at her. "I told her I was crazy about you, despite my best efforts," he said. "I told her that I loved you, and what we have is still early and new, but I'm going to see where it goes, for as long as you'll have me."

"Despite your best efforts?" Harper asked, perking her brow. "Who are you? Mr. Darcy?"

Zach furrowed his brow at the reference but quickly brushed aside her concern. "Listen, Harp," he said, sounding like an expert who just knew things most people didn't. She contained a smirk but couldn't keep the look of disbelief off of her face as she allowed him to explain his poor choice in words. "The whole love thing doesn't come easily for me. Especially after what happened in Toronto. The fact that I can admit that to you is a big deal."

"Admit what?" she asked. "I don't ever remember you telling

me you loved me. You've said you liked me and that you care about me, yes, but love never came up. And I would definitely remember it if it had."

Zach gave her a look. "Of course I love you," he told her, as though it was the most obvious thing in the world. "You made it so easy to love you, too. I'm normally guarded, is what I'm trying to say. I liked you. I liked having fun with you, but somehow, I fell in love hard and fast, much faster than I intended."

Harper grinned but rolled her eyes. "You're so romantic," she teased but leaned forward and kissed him on the lips. "I'm glad you're okay. You have no idea how worried I was when I saw them take you. I was livid."

"You and me both." Zach pressed his lips together. "I got notification that they're going to drop the charges, though." His blue eyes looked down at her, a question in them. "Why in the world would Bryan have them drop charges?"

Harper clenched her jaw. This was the part she needed assistance with. She couldn't figure out the right words to say without upsetting him. Although, judging by the deep furrow in his brow and his lips pressed into a thin line, there was a good chance it didn't matter what she did. She did something, and that was enough to set Zach off.

"What?" he asked. His voice was soft, a dangerous whisper. While he managed to control it, every now and then she detected a slight waver in his words. A hint of the temper he was doing a good job at keeping at bay. "Tell me."

"I made a deal with him," Harper said slowly. She tried to look him in the eyes as she spoke, but she only managed to get to the skin between his nose and his lips. She was a coward and she knew it.

"What kind of deal?" Zach asked. His entire body was tense. She saw the sleeves on his t-shirt twitch at the strain he was putting on it. "And don't get cute, Harper. Be direct."

Harper. He called her by her full-name instead of just Harp. This must mean he was mad at her.

"He told me he would drop the charges if I went on one date with him." The words came out rushed and tight, and Harper inwardly winced, waiting for his reaction.

Zach pressed his lips together once more, his jaw popping as he clenched his teeth together. She could feel the tension radiate off of him in harsh waves, like the ocean in a storm, and she wanted to cower, she wanted to hide, because she knew she shouldn't have meddled. She shouldn't have taken this into her own hands. She should have trusted the judicial system to do the right thing.

Once again, her fear of Bryan and what he could do to the people she cared about won. She did exactly as he told her to.

"I" – Zach began but cut himself off and shook his head. He exhaled through his nose, a violent huff that reminded Harper of a bull at a rodeo, right before he charged. Finally, Zach picked up his head and looked at Harper. "I don't understand."

Harper took a deep breath. "Bryan said that there was a young assistant DA," she explained, "looking to make an example of a rich guy who took the law into his own hands. Not that this matters, but apparently, the guy's an LA Stars fan, and their fans are assholes, so it wouldn't have surprised me if he used any excuse to mess with the Gulls' starting lineup."

Zach furrowed his brow. "Do you hear yourself right now?" he asked, taking a step away from her. "Some DA is going to lock me up for defending you just because I play for the Gulls? Do you believe everything Bryan tells you? Obviously, or else you wouldn't have stayed with him for as long as you did."

Harper felt like she was slapped and even Zach looked regretful of his words.

"That wasn't" – he started but shook his head.

"I know."

Zach opened one eye, furrowing his brow. "What?" he asked, his tone flat. "You're not mad?"

"I'm hurt," Harper said slowly, quietly. "People don't understand how impactful words can be, even when it's not their intention to say what they say. But I get that you're getting defensive right now because you don't want me going in the first place."

Zach opened his mouth, shut it, then opened it again. "I'm sorry," he said. "I've just never dated a girl who had a reaction like yours before."

"You mean a reasonable one?" she asked, quirking a brow.

"One where she didn't turn it around on me," he said. "I'm right in how I'm feeling but I made a stupid comment because I am upset that you're even put in this position. Most girls would have jumped on that comment and made me feel bad for my mistake rather than admit that they're wrong."

"I'm not wrong," Harper told him. "At least, I don't feel that way. I would have done anything to get you out of your situation. For the team. For you. I care about you, Zach. I can endure one date with Bryan."

Zach winced. "Can we not call it a date?" he asked.

Harper nodded. "Yeah," she agreed. "But listen, I need you to understand this." She locked eyes with him, and for a moment, put all of her attention into conveying a look that told him just how much she cared about him. It was hard for her to find the right words, but at the very least, she hoped he could read what she so desperately wanted to say off of his face. "Maybe I should have given his offer more consideration than I did. Maybe I shouldn't have jumped the conclusion he wanted me to. But I would do anything for you, Zach. And I felt responsible for what happened. It's not your fault that you're wrapped up in this mess. I didn't want you to be punished for my mistakes."

Zach furrowed his brow and squinted his eyes. "What are you talking about, Harp?" he asked. "How is any of this your fault? Yeah, you dated an asshole. We've all dated people we regret. That's what makes us grow. We learn from our mistakes and when we find the right person, our mistakes make us appreciate them even more. This isn't your fault. Do you understand me?"

Harper nodded after a slight hesitation. "It's just," she said, "I know what you went through in Toronto. I don't want you to have to go through girl drama here."

"The situation in Toronto is nothing compared to what's going on here," Zach said. "Just like you said you would do anything to protect me, I feel the same way about you. I don't like this, Harper. I don't like that you're doing this for me." He paused and looked away. "But you have no idea what it means to me that you would do this. For me."

Harper nodded, giving him a quick kiss on the lips.

"I'm sorry for what I said," he told her.

"You don't have to apologize," she said.

"I do," he told her. "I'm being an asshole. I just don't want him to have the ability to manipulate you using me." He breathed out a sigh through his nose. "I guess I felt responsible for that, and I was mad that he used the situation to his advantage and that you now have to go on this outing with him."

"It'll only last a couple of hours at the most," she promised him, locking her wrists behind his neck. "And then it'll be over. Then we'll be free."

"We *are* free," he told her, pressing his brow up with insistence. "No person can determine your freedom. Only you. You're free, Harper. Remember that."

Harper's heart swelled and she nodded, pulling him into another kiss, her lipstick be damned.

Chapter 22

"I DON'T WANT you doing this," Zach said as he watched her lean over the bathroom sink so she could slide her earring through her earlobe. He sat at the foot of her bed and Harper could feel his eyes on her through the reflection in the mirror.

"Do you think I want to do this?" she asked before she could stop herself. She pressed her lipsticked-lips together and looked away from him in the mirror. "Sorry. I didn't mean to snap. I'm just... tense."

"No, I get it," he said, and stood, coming to stand behind her, wrapping his arms around her waist and pulling her against him. "That doesn't mean I have to like this."

"I know." Harper locked eyes with him through the glass, leaning her back against his chest. He felt so comfortable, so safe, that she felt herself being lulled into a false sense of contentment. False because she would have to leave in the next few minutes if she didn't want to be late for their date. "I don't like it, either. I told him I wouldn't do this until charges were dropped and your record was wiped clean."

"That's not going to happen," Zach told her. "I was arrested. They'll do an arrest report because they have to.

They'll say in the report that charges were dropped, but if I ever go through a background check, that will pop up."

"Well, let's be thankful you're a hockey player," Harper drawled. She gently pulled away from Zach and he immediately pulled her into a kiss. "You're going to mess up my lipstick!" She playfully smacked him on the arm.

"Good," he said, "I want to! Remind Bryan who you belong to."

"Myself?" She raised a brow.

"Exactly what I was going to say," Zach said with a nod. He eyed her up and down and clenched his jaw. "I don't like that you're going out in that."

Harper looked down at her dress self-consciously. "It's my most conservative dress," she pointed out, and it was true. The magenta dress was scoop-necked so a hint of her collarbone was revealed. It was long-sleeved with no pattern, no other frills. The only thing about it was that it was short and tight, so her B-cups looked bigger than they already were and due to the simple black heels on her feet, her legs looked long and toned.

"I don't care if you wore a garbage bag to this date," Zach said, spitting out the last word like he hadn't tasted anything more disgusting. "You'd still be too good for the guy." He clenched his jaw and looked away. His hands gripped her waist tightly, like he didn't want to let her go. "Do you have to do this? Do you have to go?" His blue eyes searched her face, looking for the answer he wanted rather than the answer they had.

"You know I do," she mumbled, staring at his shirt. "It's harder to leave if you make me feel bad about, Zach. It's not like I wanted this."

"No, I know, I get it." He reached up and scooped the back of his neck with his hand. "I'm being an asshole, aren't I?"

"Just a little." But even Harper couldn't get her tone to come out in a teasing way.

Zach rubbed her arms up and down. "Don't worry, Harp," he told her. "This will be over soon, and then we can finally move on. The charges against me are dropped. There's nothing more that can be done." He kissed the top of her head and simply held her for the next couple of minutes. "I can always come, if you want. Like in the back of the car – or I can bring my own car. I don't mind either way."

Harper laughed but shook her head. "I don't think that's a good idea," she told him. "We don't know what he has up his sleeve."

"All the more reason for me to come," Zach pointed out. "What if he tries anything with you? I could be there to protect you. And his history…" He clenched his jaw and looked away. "My gut is saying something is going to go wrong, Harp. Please let me do something – anything. I just want to make sure you're okay."

"I know, and I appreciate it," she told him. "Really, I do. But I need to be able to handle this on my own." She paused, her eyes dropped to his chest. "I should go." Her eyes met his and the corner of her lip managed to curve up. "I love you, too, by the way."

He pulled her into a passionate kiss that lasted longer than Harper expected. When she finished, she had to reapply her lipstick, but she didn't scold him for the gesture. In fact, she appreciated it more than he could know. Zach walked her to her car and once Harper was in and her seatbelt was fastened, she rolled down the window and looked at Zach. He kissed her once again, after leaning down so he was level with her.

"Please," he told her, "be careful. And if you need me, if you need anything at all, call me. I'll be there."

Harper felt herself smile. She knew Zach meant it. "I'll see you soon," she said and as he stepped away, she rolled up her window and started the car.

It didn't take long to get to the luxury burger place Bryan wanted to take her to. It was located in the nearby mall, Fashion Island, just minutes from the beach. The temperature was still warm, so she had the air on in the car as she drove down Pacific

Coast Highway. She hoped she would find parking easily; she wanted to get this meal with over as quickly as possible.

Luckily, by the time Harper got to the mall, it was still relatively early. The lots were still almost full due to the fact that it was a Friday night, but she pulled into a spot without looking very long. Since she opted to go for practical heels instead of sexy ones, her walk to the restaurant was easier and swift. The minute she stepped through the doors, Bryan stood up from his seat and flagged her down.

The Burger Place was a ritzy, overpriced burger shack located in the wealthiest mall in Southern California. It was sleek – with white furniture and cloth napkins instead of paper – but in the end, it was still a burger shack. There was no official dress code, but for whatever reason, people dressed up to eat here at night, even though it was quite common to see surfers in board shorts and flip flops munching artesian fries during the afternoon. It was one of Harper's favorite places to eat simply because all burgers came with thousand island dressing, and theirs was homemade. It also didn't hurt that each burger was organic.

When she reached the table, Bryan pulled her into a hug. Harper stiffened but didn't hug him back. Bryan didn't seem to notice as he pulled out Harper's chair for her.

"Get whatever you want," he instructed. "I already ordered a strawberry lemonade for you. I know how much you love their strawberry lemonade."

Harper wanted to take a shower. She hated that Bryan touched her so intimately, and more than that, she hated that she let him. She wanted this over with as quickly as possible. Instead of looking through the menu, she decided to get her regular – a cheeseburger with no tomatoes, grilled onion, and extra sauce with sweet potato fries. Her eyes glanced around the restaurant. The problem was, because this place was relatively small, it was already packed, which meant there might be a delay in service.

She was just glad Bryan already had a table and put in drink orders.

Dinner went as well as it could go. She kept conversation at a minimum by giving him short, one-word answers. When the food came, she tried to eat it as quickly as possible, despite the fact that the dress was so tight her stomach might bulge from the bloat she was no doubt going to acquire. When she finished her lemonade, she politely declined a refill and didn't ask for water. At the offer of desert, she immediately declined and asked for the check. And when the check came, she made sure to pay it herself.

"I was going to pay," Bryan said, once the waiter disappeared.

Harper furrowed her brow. "There's no reason for you to pay," she told him. "This isn't a date."

Bryan pressed his lips together but didn't argue. "At least let me walk you to your car," he said.

"That's okay," she replied. "I'm a big girl and can take care of myself."

"I insist."

Harper restrained herself from rolling her eyes. Why was it that he couldn't just take her word for it? Apparently having a vagina made her helpless.

When they exited the restaurant, Bryan kept on her like he was her shadow. She pressed her lips together to keep from arguing with him; there was no point in making a scene. As the night grew darker, more and more people showed up to the mall, and it wasn't long before finding a parking spot was impossible. At least there were more people around. That should mean that Bryan wouldn't try anything stupid.

After they got to Harper's car, she whirled around. "Okay," she said. "You walked me to my car. You can go now."

"What?" Bryan asked. "No hug?"

"I'm going."

That fear started to seep into her, familiar and unrelenting.

She needed to get away from him now before he could use that fear and manipulate into what he wanted. It was one of the reasons she had stayed with him so long – his skill in manipulation, at twisting words and changing his stories just so so they weren't lies but they weren't truths. The fear indicated that he was ready to do it again. Her instincts were never wrong, and she would just give in so the fear would disappear, go away, at least, temporarily.

But she couldn't keep giving in just to ease the fear. She'd always be living with the fear and nothing would get better. She would never progress.

Something had to change. *She* needed to change.

Harper turned to the driver's side of her car so she could unlock the door. Almost immediately, she was hit with the realization that she shouldn't have turned her back, that it was vulnerable and he was unpredictable, and that was the worst combination there could be. Bryan lunged for her, grabbing her arm and spinning her around. The look on his face was hard to describe, but it was almost as though he were trying to inflict his will on her, and the fact that she was not giving him what he wanted enraged him. He leaned in, like he was going to force a kiss on her whether she wanted one or not. Before he could do so, Harper lifted her thigh and kneed him in the crotch. He let out a howl of pain.

"You bitch!" he snapped, his hands immediately releasing her so they could clutch his groin.

Harper didn't even flinch at the profanity. She didn't wait for him to drop before she slid into the car, started the engine, and pulled out. Harper refused to look at Bryan, refused to see where he was and what he was doing.

Chapter 23

HARPER'S FINGERS were still shaking as they clutched the steering wheel on the way home. She wasn't as confident as she felt back with Bryan after she fought her way out and made her smartass comment. She couldn't even let herself be okay, laugh about it, because she wanted to get home to Zach right now.

She should have expected that he would try something with her. She should have known it would be more than just an innocent date. Harper ground her teeth together, shaking her head at her stupidity. She couldn't believe she actually thought that it would be fine. After everything that had happened between them, there was no way it could be fine. It was like being friends with an ex; there was no way for her to do it.

Luckily, Bryan already had the charges dropped and he had tried assaulting her. Harper was pretty sure that if she went to the police, they would take her side over his, especially considering the fact that he had a tendency to flip flop.

Her grip tightened on the wheel as she made a left turn. The streets were relatively empty, which wasn't all that surprising. Besides the one car behind Harper, nobody was really out. It was a Wednesday night, school had already started, and she was getting into a residential area. She cracked her windows just so she could feel the soft sea breeze against her hot skin. Normally, she would have closed her eyes and taken the time to relax, but considering she was driving, she chose to breathe in deeply instead. Already she could feel the positive affect the breeze had on her body: her heartbeat slowed, her muscles eased apart, and her shoulders rolled back.

It didn't hurt that she was almost home.

Finally, she was done with Bryan.

Her lips started to curve up on their own as she imagined what she would do once she saw Zach. She was almost embarrassed at the excitement she felt, like she was back in high school and she was going on her real first date with the cute senior she'd been eyeing all year. Even though they had already been together, this felt different. It was as though Harper was finally free, and she didn't want to waste a minute of that freedom.

Sex. She wanted to have sex with Zach, and lots of it. He was something to look at and the guy knew what to do with every inch of her flesh. Somehow, he had memorized every nuance, every flinch, every breath she took when he did something to her body and she craved more of it. She wanted his hands on her hips, his mouth on her nipples, his eyes rolled to the back of his head as she took the length of him in her mouth and slowly bobbed her head up and down. She wanted to hear her name torn from his lips like he couldn't think of anything else to say except *Harper*.

Harper bit her lip as she made a soft right into her apartment complex. Her thighs were already moistening with desire and there was a familiar pelvic pulsating that she couldn't quell at just the thought of Zach inside of her. She wanted to feel him, without protection, without any barriers. It was a fantasy she probably wouldn't verbalize quite yet, but she wanted it nonetheless.

When she slid her car into her parking spot, a few feet away from her apartment, her fingers shook once more but for an entirely different reason. She gulped, trying to get her throat some moisture as she stepped out of the car with her purse over her shoulder and her keys already in her hand. All she saw was her door. A door that represented good sex and freedom.

She slid her key into the lock and turned. She suddenly realized she didn't check the lot to see if Zach was still here or if he had taken off. She wouldn't blame him if he had but she didn't think he'd do that. Just as she opened the door, a hand grabbed her shoulder. She was so scared, she jumped and let out a little yelp.

"Harper," a familiar voice said. "It's just me. It's Bryan. No need to shout."

At that moment, Zach was at the door. In one fluid motion, he grabbed Harper by the wrist and tugged her inside so he was blocking her from Bryan's view. Any thoughts about sex completely vanished from her thoughts. Instead, she clutched at Zach's shirt, clenching her jaw to keep her teeth from chattering.

Why was he here? Why the fuck had Bryan followed her to her house?

"Will this never end?" she whispered to herself.

"What?"

Harper turned to Bryan. Apparently, she hadn't said it soft enough. His eyes found hers somehow, even with Zach blocking him from view. He looked at her, genuinely confused, and that was when she felt herself snap. She refused to put up with his bullshit any longer. She refused to allow him to have such control over her emotions. She refused to be afraid of him.

"I said," she began, her brow furrowed, her voice tight, as her eyes flashed into his, "will this ever end? Will you ever leave me alone? Can't you just go away?"

Bryan still looked confused. "I don't understand," he said.

He wasn't trying to be condescending, he just lacked common sense.

"I don't want to be with you anymore, Bryan," she told him. "I don't want you in my life anymore. I don't understand why you can't understand that. I had a restraining order put on you when we first broke up. Don't you remember that?"

"How could I forget?" Bryan asked. "But you didn't renew it. I thought... I thought you were finally coming around. That you were ready to give me a second chance."

"A second chance?" Harper furrowed her brow. Now it was her turn to be confused. "Why would you think I wanted to give you a second chance? I *forgot* to refile the restraining order. That's the only reason. I thought you had finally moved on with your life. I didn't realize you needed a piece of paper to tell you I wanted nothing to do with you."

"How was I supposed to know that, Harp?" Bryan asked.

Zach took a looming step forward. "Don't call her that," he snapped. Bryan didn't argue.

"You're clueless, Bryan," Harper continued. "Sometimes I wonder if you're pretending to be this dense or if it's actually genuine. You're selfish. All you care about is yourself." She crossed her arms over her chest. "That's why I broke up with you in the first place. You were a bad boyfriend, even before you put your hands on my throat. You were selfish and critical and nothing I did was ever good enough for you. When I finally kicked you out of my life, I felt like a weight had been lifted. When you came back, I worried I would never get that feeling again. Until I realized that you don't control me, Bryan. Me and you are over."

Bryan's brow was so low, it nearly inhibited his eyes from seeing.

"I shouldn't have gone out with you," she continued. As she spoke, she walked around from Zach's protective posturing so she stood next to Zach rather than behind him. This way, she wasn't hiding. Not anymore. "You don't get to control me. You don't get to manipulate situations where I am forced to bend to your will. You are nothing and nobody to me. You don't matter. Not to me. And I hope, I truly hope, you find a girl you don't have to bend to your will in order to get your way. But she isn't me."

"Harper," Bryan began but she cut him off.

"I'm not done," she said, her nose wrinkling. "You aren't allowed in my life anymore. I don't want to see you, hear you. I don't want to breathe the same air as you do. If you ever come back to my home or harass my boyfriend or even look at people I care about, I will call the cops and report what happened in the car."

There was a moment of silence, similar to the feeling when a fire sucked all of the oxygen out of a room. Tension grew thicker, like a cloud getting ready to drop an unexpected burst of rain.

Harper felt Zach shift beside her. From the corner of her eye, she noticed him clenching his jaw, trying to control his temper. She had to hand it to the guy; he was really good at controlling his temper. Much better than she was. She could learn a lot from him.

"What happened in the car?" Zach asked, turning his stony stare to Harper. His voice was low, barely above a whisper, and tight. He was reserving judgment before he decided how to react.

Harper kept her eyes on Bryan and perked her brow, challenging him. "Why don't you tell him, Bryan," she said, her eyes hard, unflinching. "You didn't do anything wrong, right? So you should have no problem telling Zach what you did."

Bryan didn't even bother opening his mouth. It wouldn't have mattered anyway. He couldn't even look at Zach. In all honesty, Harper couldn't blame him. If she were in his shoes, she wouldn't be able to look at Zach, either. He looked at her with such fire, such hate, that Harper felt her insides wretch at the sight of it. But it didn't bother her anymore. She didn't care what he felt about her.

When it was clear Bryan was going to remain silent, Harper turned her head to look at Zach.

"He insisted that he walk me to my car even though I told him no multiple times," she said. She wasn't ashamed at what happened. This wasn't her fault. "He followed me to the car anyway. Before I could even let myself in, he grabbed me and pushed me against the car, trying to kiss me, so I kneed him in the crotch, pushed him away, got in the car, and left. I didn't realize he had followed me here or else I would have called you and told you."

Zach was silent for a moment. Then, without hesitation, he reached back and socked Bryan in the face. Bryan was so surprised, his head snapped back and he landed on the pavement of the doorway hard.

"I don't care who sees me and I don't care who you tell," Zach snarled, leaning toward him so he could look into Bryan's eyes with ease. "If you come here again, I will make you understand what it's like to feel pain. You think you're hurt now? You have no idea what I could do to you."

Harper put a supportive hand on Zach's back. She wasn't going to pull him away, nor was she going to tell him what to do. This was Zach's thing. He could handle it.

"Harper," Bryan said, his voice strained, controlled.

"You don't get to talk to her," Zach snapped, his lips pulled back into a snarl. "You don't even get to look at her. You lost that right."

"I'm sorry, Harper," Bryan continued, not even bothering to respond to Zach. His eyes seemed sincere but Harper would not be fooled by him again.

"I am serious, Bryan," Harper told him. "I really do hope you find someone who can live up to your expectations." She turned to Zach and rubbed his back in an imploring way. Without using her words, she wanted Zach to stand up and leave him be. Somehow, he understood her silent command. Bryan was still on his back in front of her apartment when she looked back down at him. "You should go, Bryan. You aren't wanted here."

With that, she shut the door, on Bryan and on her past.

Chapter 24

WHEN THE DOOR was securely shut and the lock was in place, Zach scooped Harper into his arms and took her into the bedroom. She could feel the ragged breathing, could feel his muscles twitch in response to Bryan, in response to everything that had happened. Harper wished she had some way of making him feel better but her own senses were discombobulated thanks to the conflicting emotions priming her body. She couldn't even allow herself to think that it was finally done, that she was finally free from Bryan. She had thought that before and he had come back.

Why did he always come back? Why couldn't he just move on and give somebody else a hard time? What was it about her that he needed to infect with his poison?

She couldn't bring herself to explore the question, couldn't get her rational, analytical mind working. Not yet. She was still scared, and she hated being scared more than anything. Fear made you weak and if one was weak, one was vulnerable. Harper never wanted to be vulnerable again.

"Don't say that," Zach murmured softly as he eased them onto the bed.

Harper's eyes snapped open and she craned her neck so she could look at him. She hadn't realized she had said that out loud.

"Being vulnerable means you trust someone," he explained. He leaned against the headboard but refused to release Harper. Instead, he cradled her like a bride so their legs were entangled and her head was on his chest. "It means you trust yourself. Don't let some prick take that ability away from you."

Harper swallowed and allowed his words to sink in. "You're right," she said, her voice raw due to how dry it was.

"I didn't know," Zach continued, and to Harper, it sounded more like he was talking to himself rather than to her. She gently squeezed his side just to remind him that she was there with him, if he needed her at all. "I didn't realize the type of person he was."

"I didn't either," Harper murmured. She placed her head back on his chest, sinking into his arms. She could feel his heart against his chest, reverberating throughout her ear, reassuring her that he was still here, that she was still safe.

What Harper wanted was to feel safe regardless of whether or not Zach was around. She didn't want to be a fool and assume that just because they cared about each other – just because they loved each other - meant that they were destined to be together for the rest of their lives. She wanted to be okay by herself before and after (hopefully after wouldn't exist with Zach) him. And, she knew, she would get there. It would take work on her part, but she knew without a doubt, she was strong enough to attain it if she put her mind to it.

"You never really do, though, do you?" she asked, more to herself than to him. She clenched her jaw, keeping her head on his chest and letting the beating of his heart do its best to soothe her.

"You're mine, Harper," Zach said after another long moment. He picked his head off of hers and she felt compelled to look up at him, her eyes crisp, taking in the seriousness reflected in the blue irises and the grim line of his lips. "I'll never let anything happen to you. Do you understand?"

Harper nodded. "It's not your job to take care of me, Zach," she told him, as gently as possible while still being firm. "You can protect me and you can be there for me when I need you, but it's not your job to make me feel anything. That has to come from me. And it will." She gave him a soft smile. "It should have happened long ago, but I was afraid and I didn't understand what that fear meant. Now, I do. Now I can learn from this and let it go. I can finally be happy."

He continued to stare at her. Suffice to say, she felt uncomfortable under the intensity of his stare and she felt herself shifting her weight. Without warning, Zach pressed his lips against hers in a hungry kiss. There was nothing gentle or sweet about it; rather, it was hard and possessive. Almost as though to remind himself that she really was his, that Bryan couldn't get to her again. Not with him in the picture.

Harper didn't miss a beat. She met his kiss with an open mouth, allowing him to explore every inch of it. She felt him scrape the top of her mouth, felt him clash with her tongue. Her arms wrapped around his broad shoulders on their own accord, and she clutched his shirt as though she was holding onto it for dear life.

And she was.

It wasn't long before Harper decided the shirt was in the way, however, and she removed it without hesitation. They only broke their kiss for a moment, but once the shirt was off, Harper leaped into Zach's arms and claimed his mouth as hers once more.

He caught her with ease, and she instinctively wrapped her legs around his waist. The dress gave him easy access to her and she could feel how hard he was against her already.

They needed to break apart for air and Harper immediately began to kiss his jaw, trailing fire-hot kisses down his neck. She was cognizant enough to not suck on the skin and leave a mark, but she found she considered the idea – which was strange, since she had never been a fan of hickeys before. He groaned at the onslaught her lips gave him as she tasted his skin and pushed her closer to him so she could feel his hardness even more. She sucked in a breath and threw back her head.

She wanted him.

"Take me," she instructed, her voice breathy. She only saw him through a haze but he never looked more beautiful.

Zach leaned her against the wall and dropped his hands from her waist. She used the back as leverage and squeezed her thighs to keep herself upright as Zach pushed the skirt of her dress higher so he could reach her panties. Without warning, he ripped the underwear in pieces so it fell off of Harper's body. She gasped and felt her pelvis pulse even harder. She knew she was slick, knew that all Zach had to do would be to tease her lips and his fingertips would be soaked.

"I need to get a condom," he told her, his voice ragged, rough. Almost animalistic.

Fuck. She didn't realize how much a voice could affect her body, could cause such sensations and reactions. She had never experienced anything like this before.

"No," she said before she even realized what she was saying. "Just – take it. Take me. I want to feel you. All of you."

Zach was so shocked, his grip on her loosened and she almost collapsed out of his arms. His eyes, however, darkened. "Are you sure?" he managed to get out.

Harper had no idea how he was still talking. She had no idea why he wasn't already inside of her, pounding her against the wall so hard she wasn't going to be able to walk right for the next couple of days.

"Yes," she insisted. She knew she was whining, knew there was a very immature pout on her face, but she didn't care. She wanted him. *Now.* "Please."

That was all he needed. Zach growled in response, tightening his grip on her waist. He took a moment to get her positioned the right way and shifted his weight so he could unbutton his jeans with one hand and wiggle them down enough so his cock could spring free and he could take her without any obstacles.

There was no time to brace herself as Zach thrust into her hard. She hissed in pain, causing Zach to freeze.

"God, I'm so sorry, Harp," he said. "Are you okay?"

She nodded. "Give me a minute," she told him. She could feel him stretch her out, could feel the sharp pain start to dull as she got used to his size.

He felt warm and perfect inside of her, like they were made from the same mold of clay. Like they belonged to each other and inside each other.

"Harp, I need to move," Zach told her. He was shaking, she realized, trying to keep himself contained, trying to hold onto control. "You have no idea how you feel. So fucking tight."

"Yeah?" Her eyes rolled back and she sunk against the wall.

"So fucking wet," he continued. She wasn't sure he heard her. She didn't think it mattered. "That's for me, baby?"

She nodded her head. "You get me so wet," she told him.

He grunted and, without asking her permission, began to slowly rock back and forth inside of her. She hissed, her eyes rolled in the back of her head. Her neck was starting to ache at the awkward position it was angled in against the wall but she didn't dare ask him to stop. Not when it felt so damn good.

Zach leaned forward and sucked on her neck. She wasn't sure if it was because he needed to muffle his groaning or if he was trying to leave a hickey on her neck. To be quite honest, it didn't matter. She could feel the beads of sweat stuck to his forehead rubbing against the side of her neck, could feel his biceps flex and curl with each thrust.

God, his cock was a miracle. Harper was glad she hadn't required protection. She loved the feel of him inside of her, loved how warm and firm he was inside of her.

Back and forth, back and forth, back and forth.

She arched her back and that was when he hit her in just the right way. She gasped, her lips grazing his ear. He did it again and got the same reaction.

Harper was going to release much faster than she anticipated. In fact, as pleasurable as it was with Zach inside of her, she didn't actually think she would climax since she couldn't get to her clitoris easily.

But Zach was going to get her there. And soon.

She hadn't realized she had been saying anything until she stopped speaking, until she felt herself step off that plateau, until she started to twitch on Zach's cock like she had no choice, like it was her job and she was going to earn every cent.

"Zach, Zach, Zach." She said his name like a prayer, a chant, like she was reading from scripture over and over again.

It wasn't long before Zach finished, spilling into her like a heated volcano erupting. He filled her up and didn't stop rocking until he couldn't rock against her anymore, until she took his absolutely last drop from him. His head hit her chest and she could feel his arms start to shake.

"I have to let you go," he told her, "before I collapse."

She nodded against him, her eyes too heavy to open all the way. Zach gently placed her on the floor, and her knees almost buckled underneath her. He kissed her temple before disappearing for a moment into her bathroom. She was almost positive he was cleaning himself off, and when he reappeared with a small hand cloth in order to wipe her down, she smiled.

He was considerate and she appreciated it.

"I love you, Harper Crawford," Zach murmured, pulling her gently toward him so her head was on his shoulder and so he could kiss the top of her sweaty head.

She still couldn't open her eyes but her smile widened and she said, "I love you too, Zachary Ryan," she murmured. "I love you, too."

It wasn't long before they drifted off to sleep in that position. Harper hadn't slept better in a long, long time.

Chapter 25

THE FIRST GAME of the season was always an exciting one. Every hair on Harper's body was at attention, despite the fact that she was wearing an official Zachary Ryan Gulls' jersey over a tank top and tight blue skinny jeans. The sun was still out, even at seven. Daylight savings time – where the clocks were set back an hour – had not yet come to a close so it was still sunny and bright in Southern California.

"I'm so nervous, Grandma," Harper heard herself say. She rubbed her palms on her denim-clad thighs as she watched the timer on the overhead screen slowly count down in big white numbers.

"Why are you nervous?" she asked, quirking a grey brow.

"Because you're dating the starting center?"

"Shhh!" Harper glanced around, hoping no one overheard. Luckily, the first row was typically empty at this time, with patrons trickling in during period stoppages and the first inter-mission. Usually, these people were given tickets because of the companies they worked for, who used these games as a social tool rather than because they were actual fans of the team.

Terrie gave her granddaughter a long, dry look. "What?"

she asked. "You mean to tell me no one knows about you guys? The man can't keep his hands off of you wherever you go. It's no secret."

"I understand that, Grandma," Harper said in a hushed voice. "That doesn't mean we need to go parading that information around."

"I'm just glad this is one of your first boyfriends I actually like," her grandmother said, leaning back in the blue plastic chair. "He's cute, has a good job, and doesn't call me ma'am. Also, he's charming. I like when a man is charming. Your grandfather was a charmer, you know."

Harper suppressed a smile. "So you say," she mumbled.

Suddenly, the lights went out. The rink brimmed with anticipation. Harper had no idea how but she was leaning forward, her eyes on the big screen overhead.

"Ladies and gentlemen," the charismatic announcer began, his voice ringing through the speakers, clear as a bell, "welcome to the Ice Palace, where your Newport Beach Seagulls" – here, the fans cheered wildly – "take on the visiting Toronto Bangles" – and now the boos rained down like thunder. "Get on your feet and welcome this year's Newport Beach Seagulls!"

The Toronto Bangle's starting line and goalie were already in position on the blue line. However, there was a red carpet trailing from the corner of the rink where the Zamboni entered leading toward the middle of the Gulls' home side. Harper was on her feet as she cheered for each and every player the announcer called out. They all walked down the red carpet, waving, even in their skates. A couple of players were injured, so they were announced first and they were in suits rather than their equipment. Harper saw the Gulls' mascot from the corner of her eye at the start of the red carpet, giving each player a dap with his wing. For a bird, Kenny the Gull looked like a badass.

The announcer went down the roster, with each player getting a roaring applause. When he came to Zach, the whole building was silent. There was something poignant about the moment, something Harper planned to do her best in translating the feeling into words. Toronto traded Zach for practically nothing, simply to get him off the team based on a scorned woman who couldn't take no for an answer. The divide in the team was paramount, the environment not conducive to play. Someone had to go. The management picked Zach. And now here he was, on his new team, with his girlfriend – because, yes, Harper and Zach were an item and had no problem labeling each other as such – in the stands, ready to cheer him on.

This was his moment. A moment he more than earned.

And Harper was just lucky she would be there to watch it play out.

"And center, Zachary Ryan!"

The crowd burst into applause and cheers. Some Toronto fans – there were more than Harper expected to see – booed him while others cheered him on. Harper didn't think anyone screamed louder than she did. She was on her feet, clapping her hands until they hurt, and even then she didn't stop.

As Zach walked out onto the red carpet in his skates, all two hundred and forty pounds of solid muscle, his eyes found hers and he smiled. It was the first time he had ever acknowledged her while playing and it was probably the most romantic thing he had ever done. Harper couldn't stop the elated smile from taking over her face and crinkling her eyes if she tried. But she didn't want to.

His eyes softened as they looked upon her, and the corners crinkled as his lips expanded into a brilliant grin. To everyone else, it appeared as though he was looking at something off to the side, unimportant but humorous. Harper didn't care. It meant everything to her that he acknowledged her at all, but for him to look at her like she was some special creature, an angel sent down from Heaven just for him, made any and all walls fall down like they couldn't stand a chance. She let the smile stay on her face. She didn't look away from him as she cheered for him.

She was not ashamed of her feelings for Zach. She did not want to hide them any longer.

And before he could look away, before she could lose her nerve, she mouthed the words, 'I love you' to him in a way where he couldn't mistake what she was attempting to say.

Zach clenched his jaw so it popped, his eyes darkening with a gentle seriousness Harper hadn't seen before. It meant something to him. The words. The gesture. Perhaps no one noticed it, but he realized she had publically declared her love for him and didn't care who saw.

Brandon Thorpe was announced last. As the team's captain, he had the honor of walking out in his gear with his helmet off, a Gulls' flat-billed hat on his head. Without meaning to, Harper's eyes drifted up to the box seats the Browns' had owned since the inaugural season. Seraphina stood cheering, a content look on her face. If anyone happened to look at her, they would assume she felt the same way about Thorpe as she did for the rest of her team.

But there was something in her smile, something different about it.

Harper couldn't say what, and wouldn't have noticed otherwise. However, the past couple of weeks had been illuminating. She had fallen even more in love with Zach, but her writing had gotten sharper and more tightly controlled, and Seraphina had asked her to go to lunch the majority of the week. Now, Seraphina had never actually spoken about Thorpe in a romantic way, but Harper remembered the drama that unfolded after her grandfather died, how Thorpe was suspected of the crime because he wanted more money in his contract, how Seraphina had stood by his side, despite what everyone said.

Seraphina was stronger than anyone Harper knew, and Harper wanted nothing more than for Seraphina to be happy. There was a good chance that that happiness could very well be with Thorpe, but something was standing in their way. Harper didn't know what, and it wasn't her place to know anyway, but she hoped that maybe someday Seraphina would feel comfortable sharing with her.

And maybe, just maybe, Seraphina and Thorpe would get their happy ending.

Once Thorpe skated to the back of the line, the coaches were announced. They were all dressed in suits with blue and silver ties, and they wore loafers rather than skates. It was actually amusing watching them as they made their way to their bench on the ice. The assistant coach, Brady Horne, nearly fell flat on his face. Luckily, the young coach managed to catch himself in time and wave it off as people cheered for him.

"Ladies and gentlemen," the announcer said once the applause died down, "please remain standing and remove any hats as we introduce Dawn Hasting from Tustin to sing the National Anthem and the Canadian anthem."

Everyone in the building stood. Hats were removed. It wasn't a requirement but Harper always put one hand over her heart as a tribute to her grandfather who had served in World War II. It was chilling to hear the Canadian Anthem sung by the Toronto fans. They shouted it with pride, unafraid of anyone judging them for singing. If Harper had a good singing voice, she would do the same for the American National Anthem but decided she would disrespect it simply by singing.

Once it was over, they took their seats. The Gulls' first line, including Zach and Underwood, stayed out on the ice and continued to skate. Thorpe took his stick and pushed out any stray flurry before leaning forward on his knees.

The rink got silent. The buzzer sounded. The referee dropped the puck. And the game began.

THE GULLS' won the game, 2-1. Both teams played well. Zachary Ryan, Kyle Underwood, Oscar Solis, and Brandon Thorpe excelled at their position. Zach, Oscar, and Brandon all received the three stars after the game, awarded to the best players of the evening.

Harper wrote her article that evening and sent it to Seraphina before midnight even though it wasn't due until the next day. Seraphina immediately emailed her back, requesting she come in first thing in the morning. Harper agreed.

While Zach snored softly beside her, Harper slinked off into the morning light, driving into the Ice Palace parking lot. Her eyes glanced at where that fateful press conference took place before she slid into a parking spot.

Her life changed that day and she didn't know it until now.

When Harper reached Seraphina's office, the young woman pulled Harper into a tight hug. "Your article," she said, stepping back, her forest green eyes shining, "was beautiful. It makes me realize that the entirety of last year, last season, last everything, was worth it."

Harper flushed. "Thank you," she murmured.

"No," Seraphina said, "thank you. Thank you for giving me the hope I need to run this team the way it needs to be run." She cocked her head to the side. "And you, Harper? Are you happy? With Zach. He told me how he feels about you, and I just wanted you to know I'm happy for you. Zach's a good guy."

Harper nodded. "He is," she agreed.

"I'll post this within the hour," Seraphina said, holding the article Harper had written. Harper hadn't realized Seraphina had printed it out. "Thanks again, Harp."

———

WHEN HARPER RETURNED HOME, Zach was still sleeping. He looked beautiful sleeping. He looked beautiful, period. She leaned against the doorframe of her bedroom – *their* bedroom, she realized, considering he was spending all his free time here, sleeping here, keeping a toothbrush here – and crossed her arms over her chest. Internally, she shook her head.

How did this happen?

Life had a funny way of working out in the last way anyone could expect.

And now, her heart was full of happiness and joy, love and contentment. The future was in her hands; all she had to do was act. She was free from her past and open to her future. But right now, all she wanted to do was crawl into bed with her present.

As such, she slid off her jeans and did just that. Somehow, Zach sensed her presence even fully asleep. His arm coiled around her waist and he pulled her against him. Harper smiled to herself and felt her eyes grow heavy. Zach had the day off and they didn't have any plans yet.

And that was perfectly fine for Harper.

Want to know when Book 2 comes out?

Black Eyes & Blue Lines: Book 2 in the Slapshot Series is out now! Grab your copy here!

Want updates on when my latest book comes out, exclusive giveaways, and free stuff? Sign up for my newsletter here!

Did You Like Exes & Goals?

As an author, the best thing a reader can do is leave an honest review. I love gathering feedback because it shows me you care and it helps me be a better writer. If you have the time, I'd greatly appreciate any feedback you can give me. Thank you!

Acknowledgments

This book wasn't even supposed to exist, if I'm being honest. It wouldn't be here without my betas - Angi, Cindy, Angela S., Laura C., and Summer. They're amazing ideas, insights, and edits have made this novella even better than it would be - but helped design it in the first place.

The Anaheim Ducks because they're my team no matter what.

My family

My friends

The work squad

Susanna Lynn, for your beautiful cover. It's amazing and stunning and perfect!

Frank & Kylee, Josh & Jacob, for your continued love, support, and understanding

Also by Heather C. Myers

Other Works by Heather C. Myers

Also by Heather C. Myers

The Slapshot Series: A Sports Romance

Blood on the Rocks, Snapshot Prequel, Book 1 Her
grandfather's murdered and she's suddenly thrust with the
responsibility of owning and managing a national hockey team. That,
and she decides to solve the murder herself.

Grace on the Rocks, Slapshot Prequel, Book 2 A chance
encounter at the beach causes sparks to fly...

Charm on the Rocks, Slapshot Prequel Book 3 When you
know it's wrong but it feels so right

The Slapshot Prequel Box Set

Exes & Goals, Book 1 of the Slapshot Series Most people have
no regrets. She has one.

Black Eyes & Blue Lines, **Book 2 of the Snapshot Series** He drives
her crazy - and not in a good way. But she can't get him out of
her head.

Also by Heather C. Myers

Modern Jane Austen Retellings

Four Sides of a Triangle Matchmaking is supposed to be easy. But Madeline is going to learn that love can't be planned when she starts to fall for the last person she ever thought she would, who also happens to be the man her best friend claims to love as well.

Swimming in Rain Marion is a die-hard USC fan. Aiden goes to UCLA Law School. If only college rivalries were the worst of their problems. They say opposites attract. Well, some crash into each other.

Also by Heather C. Myers

New Adult Contemporary Romance

Save the Date As daughter of a man in charge of the CIA, Gemma knew her father was overprotective. She just never thought he would assign a man she couldn't stand to be her bodyguard under the rouse of a fake marriage.

Love's Back Pocket Holly Dunn didn't know that when she began studying at a rock concert, the lead singer would call her out on it. Tommy Stark didn't know he'd be intrigued by her odd sort of ways, which was why hew invited her to go on tour with him.

Foolish Games She was everything he didn't want in a woman and everything he couldn't resist. She thought he was arrogant on top of other things.

Falling Over You She wasn't supposed to see him, hear him, or feel him because he was dead - a ghost. She wasn't supposed to fall in love with him because she was engaged.

Hollywood Snowfall It's getting cold in Hollywood, so cold, there's a good chance the City of Angels will finally get snow.

Also by Heather C. Myers

Dark Romance

A Beauty Dark & Deadly He's the most beautiful monster she's even seen

Also by Heather C. Myers

Young Adult Novels

<u>Trainwreck</u> Detention is not the place where you're supposed to meet your next boyfriend, especially when he's Asher Boyd, known pothead and occasional criminal. But he makes good girl Sadie Brown feel something she hasn't really felt before - extraordinary.

Also by Heather C. Myers

Science Fiction/Fantasy

Battlefield Just because they were, quite literally, made for each other didn't mean they had to actually get along.

Made in United States
Orlando, FL
22 March 2024

45046927R00104